Lay It Down 2

Lock Down Publications
Presents
Lay It Down 2
A Novel by *Jamaica*

Lock Down Publications
P.O. Box 1482
Pine Lake, Ga 30072-1482

Visit our website at www.lockdownpublications.com

First Edition February 2016
Printed in the United States of America
This is a work of fiction. Names, characters, places, and incidents either are products of the author's imagination or are used fictitiously. Any similarity to actual events or locales or persons, living or dead, is entirely coincidental.

Lock Down Publications
Like our page on Facebook: Lock Down Publications @www.facebook.com/lockdownpublications.ldp
Cover design and layout by: Dynasty's Cover Me
Book interior design by: Shawn Walker
Edited by: Mia Rucker

Jamaica

Chapter 1
Not My Time

What the hell is that beeping noise? Why the fuck does it feel like something's in my arms? Why the fuck can't I open my eyes? Fuck what you heard, I ain't ready to die.

"Sweets, you need to relax."

That voice, why does it sound so familiar?

"Damn, yo. You can't leave us like this."

Can't leave who? Who the fuck is talking? I tried to open up my eyes, but for some reason they wouldn't budge.

"All I want you to do is rest and get better so you can help me take care of our daughter."

"Traymon."

Just saying his name out loud caused me pain. But when I heard him say "daughter," I knew I had someone to love and live for. I closed my mouth and drifted off to sleep.

***

I could see smoke ascending from far away and the smell was out of this fucking world. I couldn't even describe it if I wanted to. I was hotter than a closed motherfucking oven on 260 degrees. Perspiration was running from my head to my damn feet.

This has gotta be hell for real, I thought.

There was a gate taller than four midgets with a big reddish black chain bolted around it. I could see people, a lot of them, too many to count from where I stood. So I walked closer. I could feel the heat even more with every step I took, but curiosity was killing me. I wanted to know who the fuck the people were.

"Damn, Black. Never thought I'd see you so soon."

"Really, Sweets?"

Even in hell this bitch was still questioning me. I would've thought she'd learned her lesson.

"Really."

She leaned her head to the left, "Guess who else is here?"

"Who?" I asked standing by the gate because I damn sure wasn't going in.

I peeked around her and saw Milk, Sham, Jimmy, Trill, Lip, Rell and Mrs. Marshall all standing on the other side. Then I noticed someone walking up to them. *Hell no! How could it actually be him? What is he doing down here with them?*

"Cedrick?" I asked as he stepped closer.

"Yes, Sweets. It's really me."

Black had a smile on her face.

"How did you end up down here, Ced?" He pointed.

"Me?" I asked, shocked as hell. No pun intended.

"Shit, you tell me, Sweets."

His face didn't hold that beautiful smile like it used to.

***

"Mommy. Mommy, are you okay?"

I've got to open up my eyes, that's my baby's voice.

When I opened my eyes, Traymon was holding Beauty and standing near the right side of the bed that I was in.

"Mommy," she cried, reaching for me. Tears were running down her pretty face.

"Mommy can't hold you right now, baby. She don't feel well" Traymon told her as the rain drop tears continued to run down her face.

"I'm takin' her out here to Regina," he said and left. Beauty's face said it all, she was hurting seeing me like that.

Damn, that was a hell of a dream. Yeah, I killed all those people, but I also killed Worm, Tammy, Damien, my father, them four Philly niggas, Alphonso, and Mr. Marshall, even though I didn't see any of them. The shit that blew me away was that Cedrick was dead and in hell, claiming that I sent him there.

I heard the door open and I looked up to see Traymon returning to my bedside.

"Stop thinkin' so hard, Sweets," he said.

How the fuck he know I am thinking hard? Is it that obvious?

"Your heart's beatin' too fast. Try not to think so hard," he said, gesturing towards the heart monitor I was hooked up to. It was beeping like crazy.

"What the fuck happened to me? I wanna know what the fuck is goin' on."

"Sweets, you been here for a whole week. You just came out of a coma this evenin'."

"Coma?"

I was trying to move my arm but my whole damn body was in pain. I swear the nigga was crying. Fuck the tears, he needed to start talking immediately.

Traymon was just looking at me and shaking his head from side to side. I was getting mad because the nigga wasn't telling me what happened. And truth be told, I really couldn't remember shit at all, other than that dream, that crazy fucking dream.

"Why you so cold, Sweets?"

I knew he was referring to my heart, but fuck showing emotions. The look that I gave him told him he better get to talking.

"Well, you know Jay is home now."

"Jay's home?"

"Let me just tell you. You might start remembering once you hear what I have to say."

Damn. This fucking beeping noise is getting on my last fucking nerve.

"Anyway, Ced and Jay are brothers. They have the same father."

Cedrick was my nigga. I met him before me and Jay broke up. Jay was locked up, and when I found out that he was seeing and sending his babyma my hard earned money, I cut his ass off, leaving him high and dry. Cedrick's dad was locked up, too. But when he got home he told Ced how he had had another child by a different woman. Long story short, he met that other child in jail. Jay.

"Jay and Ced are really brothers?" I asked Traymon, not feeling any kind of way about their relationship.

"Yea, nigga. Ain't that some shit?" He was looking at me all puzzled the fuck out.

I remembered me, Ced, and the kids going to Atlanta for a vacation because his father, Steven, telling him the news had really hurt him, especially since his mother wasn't alive anymore. But I also remembered him and his father working things out on our vacation. Steven had told him to come over when we came back from Atlanta and he agreed. We took Ced's three kids to their mother's house and I dropped Beauty off at Bella's because Traymon was still smoking boat.

Then we went to his dad's to meet Ced's brother. Ced went into the house before I did because I wanted to talk to Beauty on the phone before she went to sleep. When I opened up the door, it sounded like everyone was getting along, but then I saw Jay's face. I remembered I felt my heart stop beating in my chest. I recalled hitting the floor but not feeling it and Ced screaming "No," but I didn't remember anything else.

"T, what the fuck happened to me?"

Silence.

I was so tired of asking the same question and that motherfucker wouldn't answer for shit.

He dropped his head, but picked it up real quick.

"Calm down, Sweets," he said, looking concerned.

"Nigga, if you don't tell me, you gonna see how fuckin' calm I can get."

Every time I tried to move, it fucking hurt. My entire body was in pain.

"Word on the streets, that nigga Jay tried to lay you down."

I closed my eyes quickly and thanked God for sparing me.

"Oh yea? With what?" That I did want to know.

"A 9mm. The doctor says it missed your heart by a pinch," he mashed his fingers together.

I had to smile, knowing that Jay tried to take me out for real.

"You one lucky bitch," T expresses vehemently.

"Watch how I'm gonna freeze that nigga with his heart that he wanted to stop beatin'." I couldn't wait to get up out of that hospital.

Just then, Ced walked through the door. T's facial expression was worse than it was a minute ago. His face balled up into wrinkles when he was upset, and they are ugly.

"How long she's been up?" Ced asks T.

"She just opened up her eyes," he answered with an attitude and left the room.

Why did he lie to Ced like that? He must be still in his feelings, damn, ain't shit changed as I can see.

Ced came to my side and folded my left hand into both of his as he looked into my face.

"Baby, you had me scared to death. I prayed so hard. Then I remembered my mother's words, 'Leave it in God's hands, he'll make a way.' And a way he did make. He kept you with me, and for that I am so blessed."

Fuck what he's got to say, I hope he ain't turned soft.

"How come your face wasn't the first thing I seen when I opened up my eyes, Ced?"

He was looking dead into my eyes.

"I've been here for a week straight prayin' non-stop every day. The doctor came in and told me you had another visitor. At first I was like who the fuck could that be? So when I left the room, I seen T, Regina, and Beauty. I knew Traymon wanted to bring Beauty in so I decided to give them some time alone with you."

I saw his lips moving but my mind started wondering, *Where was Regina when Traymon and Beauty was in here?*

"I went outside to handle some business," he said, defending himself like he could read my mind, must've been the look on my face.

"You a grown ass man, you don't ever gotta explain yourself to me. I trust you, just don't ever cross those two T's together when it comes to me.

My voice was low but I knew he understood every word I was saying.

"Don't ever put that thought in your head, 'cause that bitch ain't worth a penny to me," he said while rubbing my hands.

I couldn't help but smile. I knew that bitch wasn't in my league, but I knew how weak niggas could be, especially when it came to pussy. If that bitch ever got close enough to even smell him, I swear on my life I would kill her ass, and then punish him for allowing it. Both niggas and bitches had the game twisted and I was going to be the one to untwist it, especially Jahmain Jones, aka Jay. That nigga had it coming, for real, and I put that on everything that I love.

"How long do I have to be in here, 'cause I'm ready to bounce, Ced?"

"Oh, I already know you ready to go, but I overheard them sayin' once you was up, the police had to come ask you some questions."

"I don't know what the fuck for 'cause I don't remember shit at all."

"Look, baby..."

Just as he was about to speak, two people, a man and a woman in suits, walked into the room. The lady didn't waste any time. "Hello, my name is Carmen Fletcher and this is my partner Terrence Fraser. We have been assigned to investigate this case." I looked at them and shook my head, already knowing what the fuck they wanted.

"Sir, will you please excuse us?" her partner said to Ced.

"No, he can stay," I told him. I wanted him to hear what I was gonna tell those people.

"How are you feeling today?" Carmen asked.

"Look, you and I both know y'all don't give a damn about me, for real. All y'all wanna know is who did this to me so y'all can lock them up and throw away the key. So please cut the bullshit." I had to let them know.

Their faces were priceless. At that point, the man spoke up, "We are here to protect and serve, so yes, your cooperation would help us a lot.

I know these motherfuckers ain't pushing my buttons, 'cause snitching ain't in my blood line and never will be. "Look, I ain't never been a snitch in my life, and most importantly, I hate the police."

The look on Ced's face let me know that he didn't expect me to say that. He needed to learn to expect the unexpected when it came to me. For real.

"We understand where you are coming from..." the bitch started to say, but I cut her ass off. She was a fucking liar.

"No, you don't and never will, so can y'all please leave me the fuck alone so I can rest?"

"We apologize. Here is our card, feel free to call us any time," the man said while placing their card on the table.

"Believe me, I don't need it. Now leave." My blood pressure must've been sky high because the nurse rushed in. "It would be great if they would leave," I said, looking at the police.

"Again, we apologize," Carmen said and they stepped through the door.

"If you need anything just press this button and someone will be in here with you," the nurse told me.

"Thank you," Ced said while looking at me.

The nurse left us alone in the room.

"Even in a hospital bed, you still look sexy."

"Thank you." I took a good look at him and I had to say, he was still sexy, also.

"I can't wait until I can actually sleep in my bed again with you in my arms, 'cause that chair over there ain't kickin' it no more."

I turned my face to follow his finger, "So you slept there the whole time?"

"Yea. When you was in room 918 in the coma I slept on the floor, prayin' you wouldn't leave me. I got Clap to bring me some clothes up here. I washed up in the sink in the rest room every day."

Oh, how I loved that man.

"When can we go home?"

"I'll find out, just relax, baby. I have you back now and I don't ever want you to scare me like that again 'cause I can't shine at all without you, Sweets."

That was the nigga I fell in love with. "I know I'm livin' the real life, but I ain't safe from the war that I have goin' on outside. It's just not my time to leave you."

And as always, he gave me that sexy ass smile.

Chapter 2
Get Well Time

Damn, I've been home for a week now. If I lay in this bed any longer, I know I'm gonna get bed sores. My man was the best. He didn't want me to do anything, but I wanted some dick so bad. He wouldn't even give me that.

"My chest don't have nothin' to do with my pussy," I reminded him.

"Oh yes it does," he argued.

"How?" I wanted to hear this shit.

"When you cummin', you might hold your breath, and no air gettin' to your lungs might make the heart work harder."

"Shut the fuck up," I said laughing, "Ced, you killin' me with that bullshit. You tryin' to say that you don't want none of this wet-wet," I said while putting two of my fingers inside of my pussy.

He licked his lips. "Damn, baby, you know I love every part of you, especially Ms. Kitty-Kitty.

"Well, show me, 'cause I can't remember."

And just like that, he brought me back to wonderland.

His dark eyes looked deeply into mine as he slowly placed his mouth on my toes, giving each one individual attention and sucking them softly. I shivered as his mouth left a trail of kisses from my feet all the way up to between my legs. I moved my hand to give him space to do what he did best.

"Damn it, girl." His voice sounded deep and husky. I could tell he wanted to give it to me as badly as I wanted to get it. "You've got the prettiest pussy I've ever seen."

When he put his mouth on me, it felt so good. I wondered for a second if he was right, maybe I would stop breathing, but it felt so good I didn't even care. Dying with my man dicking me down was a pretty good way to go.

He was sucking on me like I was an oxygen tank and he was a man deprived of what brought him life. He softly nibbled on my clit before working his tongue inside me while he spread my legs wider so that I was completely open to him. It felt so good. It was almost like my body wanted to close up on itself. My legs were practically wrapping themselves around his head. He pushed my thighs apart again and kept working that wonderland magic with that mouth of his until I couldn't take it anymore. I felt it building deep inside and my body stiffened as I gasped and cried his name.

"Oh my God, Ced, I'm cummin'. Don't stop, daddy, I'm cummin'."

He didn't stop eating me, but he slowed down to prolong my orgasm as he licked the juices from my throbbing pussy.

"Damn, you taste so good. I can eat you all night."

"I don't see why you can't," I smiled and caressed his cheek with one hand.

"Oh, I could, but let lil' daddy show you how much he missed you too."

He matched my smile with one of his own and my heart skipped a beat. I was putty in his hands. Whatever he wanted, he could get. He covered my body with his own and I thanked God that I was still living to experience this. He slid into me, his stroke long, soft, and easy, filling me up from the inside out. He kissed my face and brushed my hair away from my eyes.

"Be still, baby, and let me do the work."

I tried to relax but it was hard. That dick wasn't just dick. That dick was magic and it was mine. I would smoke any nigga who disrespected him and any bitch who tried to get his attention.

He was going so deep I swore I felt it in my chest. I reached around and cupped his ass in my hands, pulling him into me harder. I needed more of him.

He told me to roll over on my side and he reentered me from behind. I arched my back, slid my legs between his, and pushed back with all my might. If the heart didn't exercise then the blood wouldn't flow, right? I played with myself in the front while he drove into me from the back.

"Baby, this is your pussy."

"Oh yea? Tell me it's mine again."

"Daddy, it's yours."

"Forever?"

"Cedrick Williams, this is your pussy F-O-R-E-V-E-R," I said, spelling forever out for him.

He couldn't take it anymore, and neither could I. He slammed it to me and we both came hard and fast. My pussy tightened up around him like a glove custom made for his dick. The liquid between my legs felt warm and thick, like he hadn't busted one in months. It better had been like that too.

"Baby, I love you."

I wanted to tell him I loved him too, but I just couldn't. His own flesh and blood had tried to kill me. Even though Jay was my ex, I was only water to him, but Ced was his blood, and blood was thicker than water.

"Look, Sweets. Shit is crazy, but at the end of the day, I want us to be together forever. I know you remember everythin'," he said, while rolling me over to face him.

"I don't know why Jay shot you and I can't cover up for him, even though he's my blood. I wanted to kill him myself that night, but I knew if you lived, you wanted to handle that situation yourself. I thank God it wasn't your time to go. Yea, he's my brother, but sometimes outsiders can be closer than family, and in this case that shit is true."

"Ced, what me and Jay had is in the past. The reason why he tried to take me out is 'cause his pride was hit. I don't know if he ever loved me. But at one point, I know that I really did love him.

When his so called babyma said he was sending my money home to her, everthin' I had for him went out the window. In reality, I never knew that nigga at all."

I couldn't read Ced's eyes for nothing. He had that poker face.

"I know that's your brother, and to be honest with you, I don't give a fuck. You can either ride with me or lay it down with that nigga, it's up to you."

Ced was just looking at me, so I kept talking.

"At the end of the day, he used emotions over logic. He should have stopped to think, but he didn't and now he's gotta pay 'cause he didn't want me to see my daughter grow up. So fuck everythin' that nigga loves."

"Do what you have to do, Sweets. It's *us* against the world."

He touched my chest and I let a smile cross my face. Jay had to go. I'd already planned that back in the hospital, but hearing Ced tell me it was us against the world, made me happy.

"I love you, too, Cedrick."

***

I slept like a baby, no dreams, no worries, and I woke up in a great mood. I even made breakfast, scrambled eggs with cheese, onion, and bell peppers, plus bacon, grits, and fried potatoes. No skills had been lost, not in the bedroom, the kitchen, nor the streets. But my heart did get a little colder. Jay had to suffer one way or the other.

"Damn, the house smells good, and since you been back, it even feels and looks better."

"A mansion like this always needs to have a first lady," I reminded him with my lips poked up.

He kissed me so long and wet that my pussy was ready to go.

"Fuck me now, Ced." I pushed my body against his and felt him begin to harden.

"The food's gonna be cold."

"Shit, I haven't had any dick in two weeks. I'm ready to play catch up. Besides, why you think they made microwaves?" I asked.

He was talking shit, but we both knew he wanted it. When I turned around and lifted my skirt up to show him my phat ass, he slid two fingers into me.

"Damn, baby, you stay wet," he said while he released his manhood from his boxers with his other hand.

I leaned my upper body over the counter so he could fuck me from behind. I had to hold on for dear life when he rammed all of his dick inside me. I got up on my tiptoes so he could hit it just right. But when he lifted my legs and wrapped them behind him, I already knew I was in for a beautiful ride.

"Throw my pussy to me," he told me while he stroked my insides out.

I was throwing the pussy so hard I heard the bones in my back talking.

"Fuck me harder, Cedrick." And that he did.

"Cum with me, baby," he commanded me. He reached his hand in front of me to rub on my clit. "This my pussy, right?"

"C.E.D.R.I.C.K's pussy," I spelled letter for letter, matching him stroke for stroke.

We came together, with my face pressed to the counter and his face in my back.

"Breakfast can't be cold. That was just a quickie," I reminded him. I couldn't seem to get enough of that good dick and I didn't think that would ever change.

We ate breakfast right where we fucked.

"Sweets, you're the best. I know you've probably heard it before but, Corona, I mean it from my heart."

I knew he meant it, but if he didn't, he wouldn't live to tell another bitch a lie like that again.

"Cedrick, as long as your heart is loyal to me, you'll always have access to my soul."

I meant what I said too, it was *us* until one of our caskets dropped.

"How 'bout we celebrate tonight?" he asked.

Now he was saying what I wanted to hear. Hell yeah, I wanted to celebrate. "What you have planned?"

"We can go out, hit a few bars up."

"That sounds good, 'cause I am way overdue for some liquor."

His whole demeanor changed instantly. "So, I already see that I'm gonna be the driver for the night?" I smiled, but he didn't.

"You don't mind do you?" He was making it seem like me drinking was a problem.

"Naw."

Don't get me wrong, I was a little sore, but I was breathing, not incarcerated, and that was all that mattered. My hands were still itching and that was even better.

***

I was in an all-black Versace dress with a slit up my left leg and black and silver red bottom heels, with my hair pinned up into a sloppy but classy ponytail. I had no other jewelry but my engagement ring.

Ced was sharp as always. Polo all the way down, and I mean everything white.

"Damn, you gonna make me murk a nigga tonight," he told me with a smile. Ced getting his hands dirty? I could only imagine what his past looked like.

"Don't think I wouldn't help you."

He shook his head, knowing that I would in a heartbeat.

"You look beautiful, as always."

"Thank you, Mr. Williams, and I must say you look extremely handsome yourself."

My man was drop dead gorgeous. That's why I'd send any bitch to her maker just for speaking. I had to check Traymon's girlfriend because the bitch had crossed the line. I let her live, because that was my sperm donor's bitch. But the next time wouldn't be so pretty. I whooped her ass the first time, but next time the Lord himself only knew what I'd do.

"And may I ask where are we heading?" I was a hood bitch, but don't get it confused, I was a classy hood bitch. I knew how to act proper.

"You'll see," he said with a smile and an arched eyebrow.

**

7 was out in the cut, near the 29 and 460 interstates. I think Michael Vick owned it, but I am not sure, so don't quote me. The place was laid and packed so whoever owned it was getting paid. Michael Vick or whoever could get touched though, famous and all, no shame in my game.

We got a table by the door because I just never knew what might happen, especially since they didn't have any security in that bitch. Either fucking way, I was strapped and I hoped Ced was too. But if he wasn't I surely was.

All the bitches were mean-mugging me to the fullest. I wanted a bitch to try me because God knows I was ready. My hands were itching to pull the trigger if the bitches thought they had freedom of speech. Fuck fighting when I could drop a body easy. Niggas were looking too, but what the fuck was I going to do with a slice of beef when I had a damn bull in front of me? Ced was *everything*.

"What you want to eat?" he asked me over the music.

My chick bad, my chick hood

My chick do stuff that your chick wish she could, Ludacris blared through the club's speakers.

"You mean what I want to drink?" I leaned forward so he could hear me.

"Yea, Sweets, what do you want to drink?" he asked me in an angry tone. He was mad because I was not supposed to be drinking.

"Two shots of Coconut Cîroc."

"That's how you rockin'?" he asked, unable to keep the smile from forming on his face. He couldn't stay mad at me for long.

I didn't even answer. I rapped Ludacris *My Chick Bad* so he knew the deal. He put his hand in the air to flag down a waitress.

"Hello. What can I get y'all tonight?" she asked when she got to our table.

"One bottle of Coconut Cîroc and one bottle of Black Henn," Ced told her.

"Is that all?"

Yea, bitch. What the fuck? Don't push me, I thought.

"A bucket of ice and two glasses."

"I'll be back in just a minute."

I swear bitches kill me nowadays, I thought as she walked off. In less than five minutes she was back with everything Ced ordered. My man was money. I could even smell it coming off of him.

The DJ was killing the place. Juicy J's song *Show Out* came on, but he only played Jeezy's verse and the joint went wild. That nigga Jeezy could take a pastor from the pulpit and put him on the block with a bag of crack.

I sat back and drank while I peeped the place out. A couple more drinks and I would be on the dance floor. *Fuck it! Tonight is my night to unwind and that's exactly what I'm gonna do.*

I pushed my chair away from the table so I could make my way to the dance floor. Ced was right behind me.

Throw This Money by U.S.D.A was playing and that was exactly what I did. I threw my ass all up on him like it was money. Everyone stopped dancing and started looking at us. I gave him a little bump so I could get some space and everyone could see what I was working with.

I had a dress on, but that was not going to stop me. I did a split, let one ass cheek pop, and then made both of them bounce. I grinded my way back up from off the floor. I knew he was smiling because every nigga was wishing they had me, but he *owned* me. I danced on him like it was our own private party. I kissed him on his lips, his chin, and then his chest. I went down to his stomach and finally his dick. It was rock hard and I liked that. I worked my way back up until I was face to face with him.

Even the DJ noticed because he said, "Now that's how you treat a real nigga. What's hood, Ced?"

All Ced did was give him the peace sign and smile at me.

"Let's kill the bottle so we can finish this shit at home," I told him.

When we got back to our table, the devil was there.

"What's good, brother?" Jay said looking at Ced.

My game face was already on.

"Sweets, we meet again?" he asked.

My hand was already on my .22. I had the joint strapped to my inner right thigh. I stayed ready. I was not even drunk or tipsy anymore. My high was blown at the sight of him.

"I don't know. You tell me nigga," I said, gritting my teeth.

Ced was in my ear whispering in a low voice, "Too many witnesses."

"I see you still here," Jay said, looking me up and down.

"And when you leave this earth, nigga, I am still gonna be here."

"Don't let pussy come between us, fam," he said, looking at Ced.

I looked Jay up and down before staring into his eyes and saying, "When these fake ass niggas gone, I shall remain."

"Let's go, baby," Ced said to me.

He put three one hundred dollar bills on the table and we walked off. When I got to the door, I turned around and winked at Jay. That nigga definitely had me fucked up. Next time I knew he was not gonna be so lucky and that was as real as it was gonna get.

"Tell me you not strapped, Sweets," Ced asked when we got into the car.

"You damn right. I gotta stay strapped. I'm tryin' to make sure I get back to my child. What the fuck, am I not supposed to be ready?"

He hit the dash board hard.

"Look, don't let this nigga ruin our night. All I want to do is celebrate bein' alive, so can we do that?"

"Yeah, we can."

Lord, protect me from this nigga's family, 'cause my enemies and so-called friends I can handle.

"Let's finish our night at Fridays. We can sit down and grub, plus have a few more drinks," he told me.

He drove and we listened to Drake's CD, *Take Care*. It was pretty good. He had skills but he couldn't see that nigga Jeezy in no way, form, or fashion. Jeezy was that *nigga*.

We got to the Fridays on Timberlake Road in no time because interstate 29 was right there. Still being the gentleman he was, he opened my door for me.

It was almost midnight and Friday's stopped serving drinks at 1:30am because they closed at 2:00. There was a little crowd out there, but nothing major like 7.

I couldn't believe that bitch ass nigga Jay tried to fuck my night all up.

We walked in and headed directly to the bar. I was in need of a Jamaican lizard real bad.

"Get me a Blue Motor Cycle, baby. I'm gonna get us that table by the window," Ced said as he pointed the table out to me.

I placed my order at the bar and then walked over to my man. I heard one nigga comment, "Dayum."

So, I put a little more attitude in my step just so he could remember that walk.

"You know, you are the baddest bitch ever. With a pussy off the meters, a mind on a different level, and a *Lay It Down* finger," Ced told me once I got to the table.

The table setting was perfect, I could see the road, plus he could see his 760.

"Thanks for the compliment, but answer this, Ced. Are you strapped?"

He shook his head *'no'* and I was mad, knowing all those haters were lurking, and his ass was slipping.

When our waiter came, I ordered some jerk wings, and Ced got the Buffalo wings with fries. Shawty brought the drinks that I ordered at the bar. I drank mine down quickly and ordered another one. Jay almost fucked my night up. I had to redeem it.

Even though I was getting tipsy, I kept my surroundings in mind. I saw a couple of bitches in the corner to my right. I couldn't figure out who they were but I wanted know because they couldn't stop looking at Ced.

He followed my eyes and smiled at me. To make me feel better, he picked my left hand up and kissed the engagement ring that he gave me in New York.

Yea bitches, I am his and together we are the real Bonnie and Clyde.

Our food came, and we made small talk in between bites and sips.

"If it wasn't for my kids, I wouldn't have nothin' to live for at all." He looked me dead in the eye and continued, "I love you, and I want us to be together forever, Corona."

"Don't worry, everythin' will work itself out in due time, daddy," I told him. Then I reached over and kissed him, sealing our moment.

"I gotta go potty," I added, because that alcohol had really hit my bladder hard and fast.

The bathroom was empty so I took the last stall. I was not sitting on that seat, so I lifted my dress up, palmed my .22, and moved my panties to the side with my left hand. I swear I pissed for four minutes straight. I heard some bitches talking, but I could hardly hear what they were saying because my pussy kept spitting water. As soon as I was done, I used the hand that held my .22 to unwrap the toilet paper.

"You see that nigga Ced by the window? He look good as shit." I heard one of the bitches say.

Then someone else spoke, "He came with a bitch though."

"Fuck that bitch. She don't have shit on me."

I knew that voice, I swore I did.

"I am going to give the waiter my number so he can give it to him when he brings him the bill."

That bitch sounded confident. Just as I said, bitches could smell money coming from my man. *Haha, too fucking funny.*

"I am telling you, you shouldn't do that because he has a woman, plus you got a man at home."

I like the bitch that's talking, she got sense.

"Fuck that. I am *grown*, and who says my man's keepin' it real with me?"

She was mad and insecure.

I flushed the toilet and stepped out of the stall. I couldn't believe my eyes. I knew my ears weren't playing tricks on me. I walked to the sink and washed my hands. I felt all eyes on me. I couldn't believe this shit, my boss was trying to get my *man*.

"Talena." Me and that bitch were supposed to be cool, but I saw we were far from it. "Damn, bitch, you actin' like you happy for me, but the whole time you plottin'? You should listen to your friend, you got a man at home and Ced belongs to me."

You couldn't buy her face for a penny, that bitch was shocked. I looked her up and down in the reflection of the mirror in front of me.

"And you know my station at your shop? You can look for someone else to work it."

"Sweets, it ain't like that," her lips said, but I knew her mind said differently. Now she was begging.

"Hold your breath and die, bitch. But before you do, watch what I do." I washed my hands and splashed the water in her face before I walked out. I wished one of them bitches had the guts to try me because I was ready to leave them all leaking.

Damn, just when I tried to fix my night, I found out that my boss wanted to fuck my nigga.

"Damn, I was on my way to come find you," Ced told me when I got back to the table.

"No need for all that, 'cause I am always comin' back to you," I assured him. He smiled that million-dollar smile at me and I felt a surge of fierce love for him.

"You ready, 'cause I am. I got somethin' to show you tonight."

He didn't ask me what I was gonna show him, he just complied. He placed a hundred dollar bill on the table and we walked out together, hand in hand.

We got on the highway and I reached over to unbuckle his belt. I didn't feel like waiting until we got home. I used my mouth to start talking to his dick and it stood up straight to listen. I sucked him all the way home, but he made me stop when we pulled into our driveway.

"Stay there and don't move." He buttoned his pants, got out of the car, and came around to the passenger side.

I was barely out of the car before he had me in his arms. He picked me up and my legs automatically wrapped around him like they knew that was where they belonged and my man was where he was supposed to be. Ced put me on the hood of the 760, pulled my panties to the side, and got face to face with my pussy, eating like it was his dessert. I looked up at the sky and I smiled at the stars shining down on us. I knew that night would end in greatness. He made me come so good it made me cry. He kissed my tears away and carried me to the door. As he fumbled for the keys, I started undressing him. He started giving that dick to me as soon as we got inside. We fucked from the front door to the bedroom and by the time we hit the bed, my pussy lips were swollen like someone had taken a baseball and hit me dead in my shit. Hell yeah, I needed that night out. Now I was ready to handle business again. This city had become too quiet since I'd been gone. It was time to let them know the devil was still around. It was time to turn up the noise.

Chapter 3
Still Not Your Day

Traymon and I were taking turns with Beauty. It was my week to keep her, so I had to pick her up from school every day. I loved to spoil my little princess. She was my world.

"Ma, can you please get me some candy?" she asked as soon as she got in the car.

"Only if you're going to brush your teeth as soon as you get home?"

"Okay, Ma, we have a deal then."

I couldn't do anything but laugh because she was something else. I swear she'd been on earth before. This couldn't have been her first time.

Wayne's store was on the way home since I was taking the short way. As always, there were nothing but dope boys posted up in front of Wayne's. It was dead in the middle of the hood, so I parked Ced's 760 right in front of the store. I got out and opened up the door for Beauty.

"What's up, Sweets?" the little dope boy named Gutta said to me. He had to be at least seventeen years old. Word on the streets was he was making a nice little living.

"Shit, chillin'. And you?"

"You know. Out here tryin' to survive these streets. What brings you to the Rocc?" He wasted no time questioning me.

"Nothin' really, just passin' through. My little girl wants some candy," which was the truth.

Gutta was one of Jay's really good friends. He was young and wild, off the meter. His mom left Virginia when he was thirteen so his older sister, Tyesha, had to do some raising. Now that he was older, he was holding himself down, plus three kids with different baby moms. He must've had some good dick because he was slinging it everywhere.

I left the 760 running and the windows down with no one other than my boy Young Jeezy knocking through the speakers, with *Go Crazy*.

I got Beauty at least twenty dollars' worth of candy and I knew she was gonna be in sweet heaven.

"Ma, I just love you," she told me as I paid for it at the counter.

"Naw, princess, I love you way more."

We exited the store and I put her in the car. I strapped her in the back seat, but as soon as I turned to walk around to the driver side, my eyes locked up with Jay's.

I stopped dead in my tracks and stared Jay up and down. We were about twenty-five feet away from each other. He had this bitch named Dominque with him. I knew her because I'd done her hair down at Telena's shop a few times.

"Yo, Sweets, you still at the shop?" she asked.

"Naw, I am on to better things."

Just as she started to say something else, an all-black Chevy pulled up, and I'll be damned if it wasn't Twan. Twan was Talena's nigga. I had sold him some weed a while back when it was dry. I heard he was the main man in the Rocc now.

I got in the car and positioned my mirror so I could see behind me. Twan got out and dapped Jay up. *What a small world*, I thought. I knew Talena had to have told Twan about me and Ced. Now Twan and Jay were hanging together. *One fucking crazy ass cold world and I'ma freeze it.* My mind was racing. *Does Talena want to get close to Ced so she can set him up for Jay and Twan to rob him? Or does she want him herself?*

Either way, those niggas had to meet their maker. *Mane, I swear on everything, if Beauty wasn't with me right now, Jay wouldn't be standing, and Dominque would be screaming like the bitch she is, if I let her live.* All I knew was that nigga had to go. Just seeing him had me feeling sick. I sped off towards Grace

Street, just to turn around so I could go past them again, instead of taking my ass home. A little mind game could go a long way.

I rolled the windows up so no one could see into the car. I leaned my seat all the way back. Jay knew what type of bitch I was so he knew I was coming back. He had his hands on his hips and I knew that meant he was strapped. *Fuck him! I'm packing too, and if I give my daughter this .22, she'll be packing also.* I was pretty sure she would've known what to do with it. She had my blood in her.

I watched him watch me as I drove. I stopped the car dead in the street right across from him, fuck traffic. I rolled my window down just so he could see my eyes, and when we made eye contact, I winked at him and burned the 760's tires as I drove off. Twan and Dominque just stood there. I knew the streets talked, so I knew everyone would know we had a beef going on.

I headed home, mad that I'd let my emotions get the best of me in front of my child. That nigga wanted me dead. He'd tried to kill me, and that alone hurt me because when I looked back at my daughter, I saw that I'd come very close to never seeing her again and that tore me the fuck up.

"Ma, are you okay?"

"Yes, baby, I am okay, I just have a cold."

"Aww ma, you need some tea? I am going to make you some. Okay, Ma?"

"Okay, baby."

Life may have been a game, but it was time for a serious population decrease.

Motherfuckers better hold their loved ones close or soon they won't be within arm's reach 'cause I'm gonna do some things most of these niggas won't believe a bitch is capable of, I told myself as I drove home.

We finally made it to the Mansion. When we pulled up, Ced was outside raking up the leaves. Damn, he was sexy. My pussy started jumping just by looking at him. Fuck that, we could fuck right on top of the leaves, show Mother Nature a thing or two.

"Ma, I am going to give Ced some of my candy for Christina, Cobra, and Jr. Okay, Ma?"

I snapped back to reality when I heard Beauty's voice. "Okay, boo."

My daughter had a different heart from mine. I watched her get out of the car and run towards Ced. He dropped the rake and scooped her up in his arms. I watched them talk for a minute before I decided to get out of the car. I touched the scar on my chest and I knew Jay had to go. I walked towards Ced and Beauty.

"Hey, beautiful," he said when I got to them.

"Hey, handsome," I responded while hugging him and Beauty together because he still hadn't put her down.

He lifted my face up and kissed my forehead. "Why are your eyes red, Sweets?"

"Ced, mommy has a cold. We need to make her some tea."

"Okay, come on then, we better make her some tea, 'cause we don't want her sick."

I knew he knew better but he played along for Beauty's sake. We entered the house through the back door and I went to the living room as they headed to the kitchen. I kicked my Gucci sneakers off and flopped onto the sofa face first.

At times like that, I missed my brother, King. I needed him so I could pour my soul out, but I knew he was watching over me. I hated fucking cancer. If I could've killed that shit, I would've fired until my clip was empty and then I would've loaded that shit again.

I heard Ced and Beauty in the kitchen having so much fun. Why couldn't I have had a good childhood? Fuck it, I couldn't change the hands of time and I'd grown into a cold-hearted bitch thanks to my childhood.

"Ma, come here."

I jumped up so fast that my head started spinning for a second. Whenever she called, I was on my way, always.

When I got to the kitchen, two cups were on the table.

"Ma, I made you and Ced some tea, so can I have some juice, please?"

I didn't want any because I was not sick. "Yes you can, but you forgot the deal we had."

"Naw, ma, I am going to drink the juice then brush my teeth and play with my toys."

That child of mine was something else. Ced poured her some juice and I watched her drink it.

"A'ite, ma, I am gone," she said and put her cup in the sink.

As soon as she was out of sight, I knew Ced had a speech for me, so I took a sip of my tea. To my surprise, it was actually good.

"You can't afford to be weak in front of her, Sweets. You have to stay strong at all times, no matter what. Whatever you do reflects on her, so being weak in front of her will tell her it's okay to be weak."

Everything he said to me made sense, but knowing that Jay was still alive was killing me. "Ced, I ran into Jay today in front of Wayne's store. I had just picked Beauty up and she wanted some candy so I stopped to get her some. When I got out the store to get back in the car, he was standing a good twenty-five feet away from me with this bitch named Dominique."

"And?" Ced was just looking at me.

"We just looked at each other. Just knowin' that he is alive is killin' me slowly, Ced."

"I understand, but you cannot allow him to get to you that way. I know you're gonna make him pay, so let that emotion shit go, Sweets."

"Yo, I swear if Beauty wasn't in the car with me, his eyes would be permanently closed right now."

"Well, I'm glad she was with you 'cause you wasn't even thinkin' about the witnesses out there."

"Fuck them witnesses. His ass wasn't thinkin' about witnesses when he shot me."

"I understand where..."

I cut him off. "No the fuck you don't. You don't get it at all, I want that nigga dead," I yelled, storming out of the kitchen.

Fuck the tea. As long as Jay was alive I was gonna be sick.

I went to check on my daughter. She was the only one who could bring my blood pressure down.

Beauty's room was always in pieces, so I decided to let her play in the tub so I could clean her room up. I hadn't spoken to her father since I picked her up either, so I called him.

"How you feelin' baby?" he asked.

I hoped to God he'd quit that boat. "I hope you ain't on that shit," I said as soon as he answered.

"Naw, babyma, I just wanna make you smile."

"Beauty and my man make me do that enough."

"Where she at anyway?" he asked, playing the rest off.

"In the tub, you wanna talk to her?"

"Yea."

I went to her bathroom and put the phone on speaker so she could talk to him.

"Beauty, what you doin', princess?"

"Nothing, playing in the tub, daddy, what you doing?"

A smile appeared on my face, just like that. *No one* could make it happen faster than her.

"Aww daddy, I miss you too. You miss my mommy, too?"

"Yea, I miss your mommy, too."

That meant Regina wasn't around because his mouth was slick, or maybe he just didn't care.

"Beauty, tell your daddy good-bye and good night."

"A'ite. Daddy, I have to go so good-bye and good night."

"I love you, Beauty."

"I love you, daddy."

"Bye, T."

"Damn yo..."

He was saying some shit, but I hung up on his ass. No time for love stories mixed up with lies. Love and Lies *don't mix*, especially not with me in it.

I left Beauty in the tub while I finished her room. When I was done, I bathed her, got her dressed and told her to go downstairs. I put her in the living room to watch Dora so I could cook dinner. *Where the fuck is Ced at?* I wondered. He probably went back to finish raking the leaves up.

After 2 hours in the kitchen, there was still no sign of Ced. Beauty was still watching TV and dinner was almost finished. I'd cooked fried pork chops, string beans, and macaroni and cheese, with garlic bread.

I only set the table for two because I already knew Beauty was not gonna move from in front of the TV, so she'd eat in there.

I didn't even hear him come into the kitchen, because I was busy humming and making Beauty's plate. I jumped when he touched my arm.

"Don't be so jumpy, baby. I will never hurt you."

"I'm never jumpy, just always cautious, boo. Get it correct. Where the hell have you been?"

"Raking up the yard. Then I went and hit the shower, plus I checked the money spot," he said with his hands in the air, like I had a gun.

Instead of eating at the table like I thought we would, we ended up in the living room watching Scooby Doo with Beauty. Around nine o'clock, she fell asleep in Ced's arms. He took her to her room and I went to our bedroom to wait on him.

When he came into the room, he was ready to talk.

"Look, I understand where you comin' from, Sweets, and I respect your gangsta all the way. Whatever you wanna do, I'm behind you, but you have to be careful. That's all I'm sayin'. I want you home with me every night, because you not being here would be unbearable. I can't see Beauty bein' raised by someone else."

He was damn right, no other bitch was gonna play mommy to her, if I could help it.

"So whatever you do, Sweets, just do it. I have your back."

"Ced, we're not gonna discuss this anymore 'cause believe me I am *gonna* handle that nigga, and not just for tryin' to kill me, or playin' with my money, but for tryin' to take me from Beauty. Today is his lucky day, once again, 'cause he's still breathin'."

I walked away, too mad to talk, leaving Ced looking crazy. A shower was what I wanted right then. I needed to clear my mind. As I stood under the water, I let the words flow from my lips.

"It don't matter where you from, everything goes when you die. So I'm celebrating life, head to the sky. See I'm doing this for mines, damn right I'm gonna do the crime. No tears in my eyes, I'm forced to ride."

Chapter 4
Believe Me

For four months straight I'd been chilling, just enjoying my life, my daughter, my man, and my soon-to-be step-kids. I was taking care of home and staying out the way.

It was crazy how Ced's babies' mother don't give a fuck about her own damn children. That bitch barely even called to check up on them. Bitches like her didn't need to live at all. If it was up to me, that bitch would've been six feet deep in some shit with no flowers on top.

"Have you ever thought about getting full custody of your kids?" I asked Ced after we finished counting seven hundred fifty thousand dollars. Yea, business was still jumping and, I must say, even better than before.

"Yea, I think about that all the time, but the lifestyle I'm living is crazy, and I have no time really."

"How come?" I had to ask because last time I checked, he was the Boss.

"I want to give them a hundred percent. I don't want them around anything negative. I want their lives to be different from mine."

"I know we want our children's lives to be different from ours, but sometimes it turns out that they want to be just like us. So does that mean you turn your back on them or show them what they want to know?"

"Tell me this, Sweets, if Beauty asked you to show her how to use a gun, would you show her?"

"Fuck yea. My blood's in her."

"You crazy as hell," he said laughing at me.

"I may be, but I'm real too, Ced."

"Oh, I know, but seriously though, would you show her how to use a gun?"

"Ced, yes I would, and truth be told, I plan on showing her before she even asks."

The look he gave me was unreadable. *Him and his damn poker face. Shit!*

"This world is cold, Cedrick, the only ones that are gonna have her back is me and her father. I can't even count on him 'cause the boat's got him gone. But what happens if no one is here to show her? Then she'll already know that the only person she can trust is herself."

"Damn, Sweets. You crazy for real."

"Call me what you want to, but I want her to know that trust is very hard to come by."

"So on some real shit, Sweets, do you even trust me?" he asked, switching gears.

Damn. I can't lie to this nigga. I might hurt his feelings, but fuck it as long as I'm keeping it real with him.

"Yea, I trust you." I paused and he cocked an eyebrow at me. He was waiting for me to finish. I took a breath and said what I had to say, "As far as I can see you."

"Damn." He exhaled like he was holding his breath and looked deep into my eyes.

"Let me explain, Ced. Yes, I trust you. You haven't given me a reason not to, but we both know we're all humans and we fuck up sometimes. We even put the ones we love in danger sometimes. I'm not sayin' we want to, or mean to, sometimes shit happens. Just like Eve told Adam to eat the fruit. She loved him but..."

He cut me off by holding up his hands.

"Look, Sweets, I get the picture. I know a couple of motherfuckers have destroyed your heart, but please find me a spot in there somewhere. I want to show you that I am fuckin' different."

Attitude was all in his voice. I let his words repeat themselves again in my head. My heart was saying no, but my mind was telling me to believe him.

"I'm gonna tell you off the top, nigga, if you ever hurt me in any way, I swear on your momma's grave you gonna pay for it and you better believe me.

Jamaica

Chapter 5
Indirect or Direct?

Business was still good, and life was amazing, but with all the great shit going on, something had to fuck it up.

"I need another trap house somewhere, Sweets," Ced told me.

"Where you want it at?"

"I heard the Bridge is jumpin' hard. People say shit is lovely over there."

Traymon was holding the Bridge down but ever since he started smoking that boat I just didn't know. It seemed like it was Boat over *money*.

"Yea, shit is lovely over there, but you know that's where my sperm donor's at."

"Why can't the nigga join the team and we all eat?"

"I don't know. I can bring it up with him, but why can't you pick the Rocc, Campbell Ave, or Park Ave? It ain't like you don't have options. What about Old Forest Rd or Miller Park?"

"They're either hot or out the way, baby."

He was right, we didn't need any heat coming our way. "I'll run this shit by T and see what he says. I'll let you know tonight, 'cause I'm droppin' Beauty off with him. I have some things I have to handle this weekend." Yea, the devil was back, and she was itching to pull the hammer. For a minute, I thought I had carpal tunnel.

"Be careful." His dark eyes are full of love and a barely hidden concern. He hated when I left him for stuff like this, but it was necessary and he knew it. I'd already promised him that I was always coming back, and my word was good.

I went to pack Beauty's bag while she told Ced and the other kids goodbye. She was happy and sad at the same damn time.

Instead of going straight to drop Beauty off, I headed to Old Forest Rd for a car rental. I needed a vehicle for a week, nothing fancy, just a little something to hunt in. I already had a car in mind when we walked through the doors. I wanted the new black Impala that was parked out front.

"How may I help you ladies today?" the man at the desk asked politely. I had to look up at him. He was black as dark chocolate with braids to his shoulders and a nice smile. He was handsome, but he wasn't fine, not like my man.

"I'll be leaving town this week and I need somethin' comfortable with space to travel in," I told Mr. Chocolate Bar.

"Well, we have a variety. Do you have anything particular in mind?"

Before I could say anything, Beauty spoke up. "Since my mom needs a car, can I get some candy for free?" she asked him, serious as a heart attack. The candy jar was on the desk.

Me and Mr. Chocolate Bar smiled at each other.

"Sure, pretty lady. Once I am finished with your beautiful mother, I'll get you a sucker."

"Thank you sir."

As I'd said before, and I'd say again, my daughter was a damn trip. She needed her own world to run because I swear she'd been here before and we couldn't run this one together.

Long story short, I got that Impala for a week dirt cheap. The guy was so struck by my beauty that he didn't even ask me for my driver's license. I used a fake name.

Beauty + Money = Danger

Mr. Chocolate Bar proved himself to be a man of his word and gave my princess her candy.

I left the rental in the lot since I didn't want anyone to know what I was up to, then I drove to Traymon's house. When I was about a block away, I called T.

"Yo, nigga, I'm 'bout to pull up."

"A'ite, I'll be outside."

I turned my attention to Beauty for a minute.

"Ex'Quisite, you know I love you very much. You are my world, and I don't ever want you to forget that, okay?"

"I know that mommy, but promise me this..."

I tightened my hands on the steering wheel, 'cause I thought I knew what was coming.

"That you are always going to pick me up every time you drop me off somewhere."

"I promise, and that's on everything that I love."

Now, how in the hell could I let my only child down, especially when she had so much faith and trust in me? I loved her more than she knew.

T and Regina were both outside when I pulled up. Regina didn't look pregnant, but who knows. Bitches can't be trusted at all, 'cause they lie like rugs.

Beauty was so happy to see her father, but remembering how much he played me while I was pregnant made me sick.

"Daddy, Daddy, I missed you." Her excitement bubbled into her voice, and it made me smile. Making her happy was my only agenda, forever. I prayed to God that she endured no pain, but I knew we were living in a cold ass world, so I'd keep my heart even colder. Just to protect her, my heart would be as cold as it took.

I grabbed Beauty's bag and handed it to Regina. I wanted that bitch to say something to me so bad, just so I'd have a reason to tap her chin, again. She must've felt my vibe because she kept her mouth shut.

"Beauty, I love you. Have fun and if you need me, call me."

"Okay, ma. I love you way more."

We kissed each other goodbye, and I squeezed her tight.

"Go in the house 'cause I have to talk to your daddy."

"Come on, Beauty, let's go," Regina said, holding one hand out to my daughter.

I waited till they were in the house before turning to Traymon. "Look, T, I need to holla at you 'bout some shit."

"What's up?"

"I know you have the Bridge on lock, but Ced wants to move shop over this way..."

His face quickly shifted to sadness.

"Could y'all work together? Would you be willing?"

"Damn, you gonna let that nigga step on my toes?"

"If I was gonna let the nigga step on your toes, then I wouldn't have brought the shit to your fuckin' attention, dumb ass." *This nigga ain't listening to what I am saying. Am I talking too fast or is his ass on Boat?*

"All I'm tryin' to do is live, Sweets."

"Oh, I know, and if you wasn't Beauty's father, then your ass would be dead, nigga. I know you eating good. That bitch of yours is sharp from head to toe, plus you sharp your damn self. So miss me with that tryin' to live shit." I called it how I saw it.

"So, I guess that means no, and you ain't trying to get on my team then?" I continued.

"What the fuck I look like workin' for my babyma's nigga?"

I'm gonna have to school this nigga like a child. "Money, nigga, M.O.E. You're gonna look like fuckin' money. That's where your ass fucks up at. You don't know how to communicate with Real Bosses. You act like you wanna be a fuckin' part-time hustler who smokes Boat for a livin'." I knew I hit a nerve with that, but fuck it the truth always hurts.

"I'll be that," he said with a laugh. "But I'll hold my side down by my damn self."

"Look, I'm gonna be as direct as possible. Be glad that Ex'Quisite is your child."

I got in my car, but he walked to the passenger side window, so I let it down.

"And why is that?" he had the nerve to ask me after I'd just told him a minute ago.

"Cause she's keepin' you breathin'. I can't get more direct than that."

I pulled off, bumping none other than my boy, Young Jeezy.

"This one's for you and I ain't talkin' bud lights,
H.K. nigga with the little red lights,
Whole club bouncin' everybody strapped up,
Pull it out my pants and make everybody back up,
Fuck a record deal your boy just too real..."

Jamaica

Chapter 6
Clock Tickin'

I parked my car on Hill, a back side street just to be on the safe side. I took a cab to Enterprise to pick up the Impala, because it was time to make some moves.

First, I rode out to Jay's mother's house on Sussex. I camped for an hour, but no one came or left, so I left.

"I'm gonna find you, Jay," I said, like he could hear me, even though I knew he couldn't. "I'm comin' for you, nigga. Your time is runnin' out.

His baby's mother's house was next on my list of places to go. That run down bitch lived with her grandparents on Lindsay, which was a dead-end street. As I turned onto the street, I saw her on the porch with the baby, but no sign of Jay playing daddy.

On everything I love, the baby didn't look like Jay at all. That bitch was looking at my Impala so hard I could tell her head must've been hurting because she was so busy trying to figure out who was driving it. The windows on the Impala were dark as shit. I knew those lame ass police officers would fuck with me if they were bored so I left my strap in the other car. Going to jail for a gun would get in the way and was not on my time.

I turned the car around and sped back up the street. *Ugly ass bird brain bitch*, I thought as I drove past her. *How far could Jay actually be? I mean, damn, Lynchburg ain't that big.*

I went straight to Wayne's store next because that was the last spot I'd seen him at. When I hit the corner by Wayne's, all the dope boys took off running like track stars. They were thinking I was the boys in blue undercover. But still there was no sign of Jay, so I was gonna ride by his sister's house next.

Lauren was cool as shit, a real down ass bitch with a worthless baby daddy. That shit was so sad and I thanked God that wasn't a part of my life. I could be daddy and mommy in one if I had to. Traymon was lucky that Beauty loved the ground he walked on, because I was ready and willing.

I whistled when I pulled onto her street and saw what was in her driveway.

"When the fuck she get herself an all-black Chevy?"

I knew good and damn well she wasn't riding that clean. I wanted a closer look. As I got close enough to see clearly, I thought my eyes had to be playing tricks on me.

A smile came across my face when I realized what I was seeing. Twan and Jay were hanging close together. I parked five houses down with Lauren's house in sight. I had to get that nigga's schedule down. I couldn't keep letting his ass get away from me. I knew those niggas might even plan on plugging me themselves.

I called Ced to see what he was doing and to let him know that I was okay.

"Baby, what you doin'?" I asked him in my sexy voice.

"Nothin', just cleanin' this kitchen up. Cobra wanted to cook so I let her do her," he said with a good laugh. I liked the sound of pride in his voice. He loved his kids.

"For real? What did she cook?" I had to know. I hoped she had thrown down with her little seven-year-old self.

"Some French fries and eggs."

"French fries and eggs? She made French fries and eggs?"

"Yea, baby. You know kids eat the craziest things. It actually tasted good."

That cracked me up. He still had that kid side to him.

"What you laughin' at?"

"Papi, you are somethin' else."

"Hurry up and get home so I can show you somethin' else."

"Oh, don't worry, I'll be home soon, daddy."

"A'ite."

I hung the phone up just in time, because I'd be damned if those lame ass niggas weren't leaving together. Jay was getting in the driver's seat and Twan was on the passenger's side. Jay didn't have a license and he was pushing an all-black Caprice with 24's on its feet and "NO SLEEP" on the license plate. The fuck boys were already ready to pull them over just for driving while being black. Nigga's don't use their heads for nothing, not for money, not with cars, not with pussy, *nothing*.

They pulled away and I waited for about ten seconds before I followed because I had a gut feeling the light at Burger King was gonna catch them, and it did. The light was red and I could hear their music clearly, even from a few cars back. Stupid ass niggas were practically calling the police towards them because they were trying to stunt. I wasn't hating, but stunting without a license, especially in this city called Lynchburg, was outrageous.

Twan's got a license, why ain't he driving? I wondered.

Traffic was flowing. I was four cars behind them and wondering where the fuck those niggas were going at 7pm. I had all night to see anyways, so I was down to ride.

They turned into Liberty gas station on Campbell, but I kept straight and signaled to turn on Otis. Then I made the first left. I cut my lights off and parked the car. I could see the store from where I was and the view was good. The Chevy was parked at the gas pump, so maybe they were low on fuel. I let my window down a little in case I could hear if they were talking. As long as nobody was bumping too loud, I would be good.

A purple Maxima pulled up with nothing but females. I give props when props are due, but those bitches looked atrocious. I saw Jay exit the store, and Twan was two seconds behind him. I couldn't even lie, those niggas looked good, but fuck looking good. I was in this for retaliation.

"Damn, y'all look fly," I heard Twan telling the bitches.

Niggas would lie to get different pussy. Sad world, true story. Jay was pumping gas when I heard him holler, "Them dusty ass bitches ain't shit."

A smile crept across my face because he wasn't telling nothing but the truth. Twan got in the driver's seat, so I knew for a fact they were getting ready to show off, or at least try to.

Talena better enjoy that nigga while she's got him, 'cause he's gonna be wiped out soon. Their system was so loud, I could've sworn they had a midget in the trunk beating on shit. They had the loud horn on too, so everyone could hear the words clearly outside. I wasn't trying to hear no Lil Wayne, so I rolled my window up and pushed play on the CD player. Meek Mill was killing the music scene at the time. He was hungry for the music and, since I was hungry for Jay's blood, I let Meek Mill's *Dreams and Nightmares* bump through the speakers.

When they pulled out of the gas station, they made a left. I made a left, stopped at the stop sign, then made another left, and I was right behind them. It wasn't that much traffic, so I had to be careful. I put my fitted hat on and dropped my seat all the way back so it looked like a nigga was driving.

Instead of going straight to Park Ave, they turned left by Virginia College to get to Memorial. Everything they did, oh you better believe I did it too. Crazy how motherfuckers don't pay attention to their surroundings. Fuck it, I ain't them and they damn sure ain't me. They were driving around doing nothing, and knowing Jay, that nigga was strapped the fuck up. If the police pulled them over, I knew for a fact Jay was gonna be hauling ass like that Jamaican runner, Usian Bolt.

We were on one of the hottest streets in the Burg, Warths Worth. They were way ahead of me, which was cool because I didn't want them to know I was on their asses. Suddenly, their brake lights came on.

"Why the fuck are they stopping?"

I couldn't just stop and park that quickly without looking suspect so I kept going straight. They parked the Chevy on the left hand side, and by the time I drove past them, I saw a couple niggas by the door.

"Who the fuck live over here that they know?"

I made the next right and ended up over on Miller Park, where I parked the Impala. At times like that, I needed someone to walk around the block and check shit out.

"Fuck." I punched the steering wheel, mad as hell. I wondered if the niggas knew that I was following them. So many thoughts were running through my head.

"Come on, Sweets. Get yourself together."

There's an old saying that goes, "You can always ask yourself a question, just don't answer your own question." I had to laugh at myself because those niggas had me tripping the fuck out. I took a long pull on some fresh air and then I exhaled slowly. *I got this*, I silently told myself.

I put the car in gear and pulled out to drive back over to Warths Worth. I hadn't come this far to just drive away. It was too late for that.

That proved to be perfect timing. As soon as I turned onto the block, those niggas pulled out right in front of me. I had almost hit the back of the Chevy.

"What the fuck?" I threw my hands up.

Twan threw his hands up too. I figured he was saying he was sorry, not knowing who he was saying it to. I was bumper to bumper with them and I could see what they were doing. Just the two of them, going down the block towards 7/11. They were passing something back and forth. I could have bet my last dollar that it was a blunt.

Damn, what the fuck is up with these lights tonight? I thought as the light by 7/11 caught them, which meant that I was caught too.

Their signal came on, they were going right. *Shit, I'm going right too. Six, five, four, three, two, one,* I counted down to put some space between us before I turned.

We were going down Ford Avenue. The only thing to do on a Friday night was hit the bar, and Ford would have led us there. I'd be damned if the light by the stadium wasn't red, so I switched to the left lane.

"Please change, I am begging you." I was talking to the damn light. I was losing it for real. Just as soon as I hit my brakes to slow down, the light changed.

"Hell yeah," I said out loud.

My passenger window was cracked and, with no music coming out of my speakers, I could hear the sounds of other cars. Twan's Chevy had to have a turbo motor because every time he hit the gas, his twin pipes started talking.

Ford Avenue would take us to either Timberlake Road or Wards Road, plus there were side streets. I gave the Chevy some space and stayed my ass in the left lane. I noticed Twan signaled to turn right.

"Lindsay Street? What the *fuck?*"

Jay must've been going to see his so-called baby. I put my signal on and turned left, grateful the Waffle House and Walgreens were right across the street from Lindsay. I pulled into the Waffle House and parked facing my targets.

I couldn't believe that Jay came home and started fucking that bitch again. That was the same bitch him and his niggas ran a train on, the same bitch with the same pussy that left him for dead, but the craziest shit ever was that she was the one who called the police on him. I wasn't God so I couldn't judge, but what would I have looked like fucking with a nigga who'd called the police on me?

I couldn't even believe myself because, truth be told, I'd let my heart get the best of me with that nigga. Now he was back out here fucking with the raggedy pussy ass bitch De'Bonye again.

Jamaica

Chapter 7
Whatever Floats My Boat

Jay's sister, Lauren, and I used to speak every time we saw each other. Jay knew who I was, and I knew who he was, only thing was I'd never said a word to him. Lauren came up with this great idea one evening while I was doing her hair.

"Sweets, my brother said 'What's good?'"

"Bitch, you know I ain't ready for no relationship. I have a child to raise."

"Bitch, I know this. You don't have to rush shit anyway," she said.

"Why?" I asked her, kind of puzzled by her answer.

"Jay got locked up so this can give you some time to get to know each other, through pen and paper, phone, visits, I mean whatever."

"Damn. What the fuck's he locked up for?"

"You wanna know the truth, Sweets?"

"What you think?"

"Well he was fucking this bitch, De'Bonye, well him and his niggas was. De'Bonye's best friend Tunkie started fucking with Jay on the side, so De'Bonye gets mad. Every time De'Bonye and Tunkie see each other, they fighting. No matter where they at, they going at it, full force. Jay went to a party one night in the Rocc and ended up shooting this nigga named Fresh in his ass. The bitch De'Bonye seen the shit and reported it to the police for a thousand dollar reward. She did that shit 'cause she knew Jay would get locked up and that meant that he wouldn't be fucking anyone anymore. The nigga Fresh wouldn't even talk to the police. That nigga kept the street code of loyalty alive. When the boys in blue ran up on Jay a few weeks later, they found the .45 he shot Fresh with, but they couldn't charge Jay with nothing but having a gun while being a convicted felon. Long story short, they gave him almost three years, thanks to that damn lawyer I am still paying for," she said laughing.

"Damn, that's crazy," I told her.

"Well, I told him I couldn't give him your number until I talked to you. So now that I've told you, can I give it to him?"

"Yea, do that."

I didn't see any harm in that. The least I could do was help and encourage him to keep his head up. The next day, that nigga called me on a three-way.

"Hello?"

"May I speak to Sweets?" the female voice said into the phone.

"This her."

"Hold on, my son wants to talk to you."

I waited.

"What it do ma?" he said as she clicked over to connect us.

"Who the hell is this?"

"Jay, Lauren's brother.

"Oh, hey, how are you doin'?"

"Good, now that I am talkin' to you."

That made me smile.

"Oh really, how is that?"

"I been tryin' to holla at you but our timin' wasn't right."

"Really?" *Niggas will tell you anything while they locked up,* I thought.

"I hope I didn't catch you at a bad time or anything?" he asked.

"Naw, you good."

"I don't want your nigga to start trippin' on you or anythin' like that."

"If I had a nigga, you wouldn't be on my line right now. Plus, I am a grown woman. I can do what I want 'cause I am the Boss of me."

"Oh yea?"

"Oh yea, you heard me. " *He must not know.*

"I like that."

"I bet you do." *Who wouldn't like a Boss Bitch?*

After that phone call, we were like one. I started sending money and putting money on my phone so he could call straight through. I was sending stacks of mail every day and even going to visit. I fell in love with him like that. We never had sex, the most we ever did was kiss and touch a little. Unless you count phone sex, but that was all. I fell in love with him, not knowing it would be all lies. He'd told me all about De'Bonye and the baby from the jump.

He had my pussy on lock from behind bars. I knew that was crazy, but he had my heart on cloud twenty, had me dreaming about how we would make love on his first day out. The nigga had me wishing for a picket fence and a big belly.

Then I met Ced, but the whole time Jay had his so-called baby-mama on the side. Not only was the bitch going to see him, but he was sending her my hard-earned money. Then the motherfucker came home to learn that Ced was his brother and I was Ced's fiancé. But what put the icing on the cake was that the nigga tried to take me out of this world right in front of Ced.

"How fuckin' dare him?" I said out loud.

I'd been brooding on that shit, but I was finally back to reality. Jay had to receive a painful death for what he'd done to me. My heart had grown too cold for him to just walk away and keep living like he deserved life.

I pulled the visor down and looked in the mirror. My reflection said it all. The pain in my eyes was an echo from my heart. There was no passage of light or hope, my heart was nothing but frozen ice, just because I let love get the best of me. They said it was a thin line between love and hate, but they were wrong. There was only death between love and hate in my world. Everyone that hurt me always paid and, in due time, he would also, because that was how my boat was gonna float.

Chapter 8
Get Back On Track

I shut the visor in time to see the Chevy pulling back onto Ford Avenue and heading towards Timberlake. I hit my lights and exited the parking lot. They were only ahead of me by a little bit. I was close enough to see the flat screen come down. I couldn't see what was playing. What really interested me was that I only saw one shadow inside the car. That meant Jay probably stayed on Lindsay with that retarded looking, run down pussy bitch, De'Bonye.

Knowing that she was getting the dick had me sick. Don't get it twisted, Ced had a remarkable dick, but how was Jay's? I'd waited almost two years for that shit, but I would never know how it was.

I followed the Chevy all the way to Friday's, but I parked at Kroger and watched as Twan got out of the car. I knew it was Twan because Jay's walk was completely different. That nigga was going to get white boy wasted.

I decided to head home to my man. That mission wasn't hitting on shit.

I dropped the rental where my Lexus was parked and headed home.

Twan and Jay were new best friends and Jay was back fucking with De'Bonye. It all had me at a loss for words. I knew I had to get back on track and stay there.

Jamaica

Chapter 9
Da Truth Shall Be Revealed

Two weeks had gone by and I must say Jay and Twan were acting more and more like brothers. My surveillance on those niggas was top notch, and come to find out, Twan was providing Jay with work, but what made the pie sweet was that Jay and Regina were messing around. I'd told T that bitch was a hoe from day one, but hey, he wanted to turn a hoe into a house wife. Now that bitch was fucking with Jay, and she needed to be stopped. I checked that hoe with an ass beating when she tried to holla at Ced, but what she needed was to be buried.

I put T up on game about Regina, and his pride was crushed ecause he fucked us up for a low down hoe. The joke was on him.

"Look, tell that bitch you goin' out of town for a couple of days to handle business."

"A'ite, I got you."

I knew he hated taking orders from me, but I wanted him to see that shit for himself. He must've wanted to see it too, because he let it ride. Crazy how the tables turned, but Karma was an ugly bitch, and she just kept coming around.

On Thursday, T, Beauty, and I decided to chill together and figure some shit out. I picked him up from the Greyhound bus station in my black Impala.

"Damn, nigga, you stay ridin' clean," T complimented me on the ride.

"Daddy, you didn't know that my mommy is a *boss*?" Beauty asked him from the back seat.

I almost choked on the Pepsi that I was sipping on. T and I looked at each other and smiled. The way Beauty was thinking let me know that one day she wanted to be a boss her damn self because she was paying attention.

"We have us a room at the Hampton Inn, so call and see what she's doin'."

"I'm gonna call her once we get to the room," he said to me, and I knew that was his way of saying he wouldn't take too many orders.

We got to the hotel in ten minutes flat. I already had the room reserved.

I watched Traymon step onto the patio with his phone in his hand as I used my own to call Pizza Hut and order a pizza for Beauty. When that was finished, I called Ced.

"Hey, daddy."

"Hey, Mrs. Williams."

I loved it when he called me that. It put a smile on my face every time.

"I miss you too, girl," he said to me in a sexy tone that made my stomach flip over on itself. Even through the phone that man got to me.

"When are you comin' back, 'cause I am in need of some of that good dick?" I whispered into the phone, because Beauty was always in everyone's conversation. Ced was out of town with his right hand man, Clap.

"Soon, don't worry. Where's Beauty at?" He must've been thinking the same thing.

"She's right here with me watchin' TV."

"Oh, ok."

"Well baby, I ain't gonna hold you up. Just call or text me when you free."

"A'ite. I love you, Sweets."

"I know you do, Ced, and I love you more." I ended the call.

Traymon walked up on me as I was daydreaming.

"You love that nigga, don't you, Sweets?" I heard regret in T's voice.

I looked at Beauty and smiled. "I love me some Beauty," I said as I walked towards the bed. I wasn't gonna hurt his feelings no more than I had to, so I ignored his question.

I picked Beauty up off the bed and tickled her until she couldn't take it anymore and begged me to stop.

"Ma, ma, you play too much," she squealed as she tried to catch her breath.

Bam. Bam.

Someone was knocking on the door. I touched my waist to make sure my best friend was there, my 45.

"Who is it?" I yelled.

"Pizza delivery," a male voice hollered back.

I fixed Beauty a plate and put her back in front of the T.V. because she was on that Dora the Explorer. T and I headed to the patio to talk.

"Damn, I wish shit was different, Plum. I wish it was you and me together, raising our daughter. Could that ever happen?"

He hadn't called me that in years. Plum used to be his nickname for me, but I guess I wasn't sweet enough because he left me. I can't even look at him. I kept my eyes on the parking lot.

"I don't know what the future holds, I don't even know if I'll live to see tomorrow, T, but what we had, we had. You, T, you traded us for that shit you puttin' up with now."

What I thought but didn't say was, "You deserve it."

"How can I ever get back what we had, Sweets? How can I make you happy again? How can I rewind time and go back?"

His words unexpectedly touched something in my heart, but how could I ever choose him over Ced? The conversation was getting uncomfortable.

"Look, just live your life. Live it for you and Beauty. What we had is gone. You have hurt me so bad, you'd never imagine how many nights I cried myself to sleep. I thought life was unlivable without you, T." My eyes were locked onto the road.

"Sweets," he said, reaching out to touch my arm.

I didn't pull away. I turned to face him and we locked eyes with each other.

"I love you. I've never stopped loving you. I am still in love with you and no woman could ever get my heart or my soul. They both belong to *you*, Corona Cocaine Cash, and that's on everything I love. I might have shown you the wrong way back then, but I promise you I know how you want to be treated now and I can show you, Sweets. Let me show you."

I'm not good at dealing with other people's emotions. I don't have too many of my own, but I had to wonder if that was the desperation of a nigga on the rebound seeking comfort in what he already knew, or had he really always loved me? It didn't matter. Fuck what he was saying.

"T, we gonna leave that situation alone and handle this problem with your bitch and Jay." I had to brush that shit off. Emotions could cause errors and I couldn't have that.

"Damn, that's how it is?" He looked surprised. I didn't know what he'd expected, shit!

"That's how it's gotta be. You made it like that, Traymon. We all gotta bear the consequences of our actions." I left him standing on the patio.

The room wasn't bad. There were two twin size beds, a brown desk, a T.V., and a bathroom for sixty-five dollars a day. That was a deal, but the carpet was ugly as sin.

Beauty was still watching .T.V. but she seemed tired and restless.

"You want to lay down, boo?" I asked her.

"Yes ma. Can I?"

"Sure, baby. All you have to do is pick a bed."

"Where you and daddy going to sleep at?" I should've known that question would come from her. "Who do you want to sleep with?"

"It doesn't matter, ma."

"Ok. I'll sleep in the bed with you, and daddy will sleep by himself."

Me and him in a bed together? Hell no.

"Ok." Her voice said nothing but hurt. I knew she wanted us back together, but I would not allow that to happen. Never.

She got in bed and positioned herself so she could still watch T.V. I left the room and went back out on the patio to see what Traymon was doing.

"Damn, it's almost 7pm already." He had his head down looking at his shoes.

"How do you figure that?" I asked him.

"'Cause I just looked at my phone," he responded. His voice was damn near toneless.

"Did she even text you yet?"

"Yea, claimin' she's goin' out with her cousin Erica. That bitch Erica is nothin' more than a low down hoe. She tells me that she's pregnant, but she's not ready to have a baby yet.

"And let me guess," I said. "You ready to have another child?"

"Sweets, I don't even know. I just wanna be happy."

I had to look at him to make sure he was not crying. "In due time you will, Traymon."

"Easy for you to say," he scoffed at me.

All I could do was shake my fucking head and look ahead of me.

Nigga, I thought having me in your life completed it, but I didn't. Now you're gonna see for yourself that Karma is for real.

"Let's go inside 'cause the show's about to start," I told him.

He gave me a look like "What the fuck," but he did what I said.

We went inside and closed the curtain that covered the patio door.

Beauty was fast asleep so I cut the lights off, but I let the T.V. watch us, same as always. I glanced at my phone, 7:02pm. I pulled Traymon to the window and showed him his hoe in action.

For the past two Thursdays, Regina and Jay had been coming to the hotel. I didn't have any facts about what they were there for, but I was no dummy, and I had my suspicions.

His face was priceless. He squeezed his temple with his left hand.

"This bitch been playin' me, Sweets."

No shit, nigga, she's a snake in the grass, same way she got you, that's the same way she'll get another.

"Shhh... Our daughter is sleepin'."

"Damn, all this time, I thought I had me a dime, but now I see I don't even have a penny."

Now he was coming to his fucking senses.

"That's your precious Regina with Jay." That bitch loved my leftovers.

"Mane, I am gonna kill that bitch," he said through gritted teeth, but actions speak louder than words.

"Be careful of what you say Traymon." I'd already killed that bitch in my head.

"Naw, I'm serious, Sweets. I'm gonna kill her ass."

I looked at Beauty to make sure she was still sleeping, and I hoped she was not just lying there. "What they doin'?" I asked him.

"She's gettin' out the car now, I think he just got back from the front desk. This shit is real." He rubbed his eyes like he wanted to make sure that what he was seeing was correct.

"Now they goin' to their room, I guess." The pain in his voice said everything that his words didn't.

"Don't worry, Traymon. They're both gonna pay."

"You ready to go?" he asked me.

I guess that was too much for him in one night.

"I'm always ready. Grab Beauty and let's go."

He picked Beauty up, kissed her face, and gently placed her over his shoulder.

"Will they see us?"

"Naw, they gettin' the last room at the end, T."

I could've sworn I saw a tear run down his left cheek.

"A'ite, let's bounce," he said without questioning me.

He was learning. His face said he was gonna hurt her, but I had something better for her and Jay. I just wanted him to see them both with his own eyes. Once we got into the car, he spoke first. "Just drop me off in the hood."

"You sure?"

"Yea, I'm sure, Sweets."

Don't get mad at me, nigga. We didn't say anything else. Young Jeezy's was the only voice in the car.

I guess this is what it feels like when you're royalty, homes
And you wake up and the loyalty's gone
Them short sentence niggas come on yeah, feel in the way
Same niggas that were hating back then, still in the way
I swear these niggas think my life is just bitches and Champagne...

***

Finally, we made it to his hood.

"Kiss Beauty for me, babyma."

"You know I will. Keep that snake ass bitch close to you," I told him as he got out.

I could see the hurt in his eyes, but all I could think was what I always said, "Karma is a bitch."

Jamaica

Chapter 10
Bitch

I was back.

"Beauty, you're going to stay at Bella's house for a couple of days, ok?"

"Ma, but you're going to come back to me, right?"

"You know I'm always comin' back to get you, baby," I told her as I kissed her face.

I packed her bag as she watched Dora.

"You ready?" I asked her twenty minutes later.

"Ma, you know I stay ready, just like you."

Her comment caught me off guard, but as I looked at her, I knew she would be just like me when she got older, or even better. "Let's go then."

As we rode to Bella's house, I couldn't help but to think about Dimples.

Damn, I truly missed her, but how could I find her, and if I found her, what would happen next? Could we ever be friends again or would I have to kill her? Did I really want to know? Dimples was my dawg, we had so much love between us, and I never dreamed it could've been broken, but pussy and the disloyalty that came with it was what broke us up.

In a way, I felt like whenever we did see each other again, it was going to be war because once someone betrayed me, I was probably gonna kill them. Loyalty was a must in my life. I would allow no one to cross me or the ones that I loved because I was going to get them. It might not be immediately, but eventually I would. I waited patiently for years before being able to pass my own judgement on those who hurt me as a child. I knew how to wait.

"A'ite, Beauty. I am going to call you every day, but if you need me first, all you have to do is tell Bella to call me, okay?"

"Ma, I love you with all of my heart."

"I love you way more, baby girl, way more."

"Ok."

I had a bad feeling that someone was watching me, and I was not going to brush my instincts off like that. I trusted my gut, and I was going to be paying much more attention to my surroundings.

I hadn't heard from T in two days. I hoped he hadn't smoked himself to death, but knowing him, he was probably high on boat right about then.

"Yo, nigga, what you doin'?" I asked when he answered his phone.

"Nothin', babyma, just chillin'. What you doin'?"

He didn't sound high because his words weren't dragging. The nigga slowed down when he was smoking boat.

"Shit, just doin' me. I just wanted to make sure you was okay."

"I'm straight. Thanks for checkin' up on me."

"You know it's all love." That was what real bitches did. I didn't love him, it was just the point of showing him I cared about his feelings, because of our child.

"A'ite, I'm out."

I ended the call and put my phone between my legs.

Twan and Telena lived on Shaffer, 1625 was their address. I rode by, but I didn't see either of their cars in front of their house, so I left.

The next stop was home. I hit highway 29 and let Young Jeezy's *Go Crazy* talk to me.

My mood was interrupted by my cell phone.

"Yo, where you at?"

"On my way to the spot, why you sound like that?"

"Mane, some lame ass niggas tried to wet me up." He was out of breath.

68

"Where you at?" I asked him, instantly concerned.

"I'm on Polk Street, behind the Beauty Salon."

"A'ite. I'll be there in a second." *Damn, that nigga better be ready to ride 'cause I am in go mode.*

I hit the first exit off the highway and put the Impala to the test. I pulled up at the Beauty Salon. I still had him on the phone so I told him to come to the front.

I could hear the police sirens coming from a mile away.

"Damn, Sweets, when you got this?"

"Ced, this isn't exactly the best time to ask me about a car. We gotta move." I pulled out of the parking lot, trying to put space between us and the scene. I watched him as he checked himself by rubbing his body down with his hands.

"Damn," He yelled and hit the dash board with his fist.

"What the fuck is goin' on?" I needed to know as I hit the exit.

"Mane, I hope Clap is straight."

"What the fuck is goin' on?"

Before he could answer me, his phone went off.

"Yo, my nigga, you good?"

I couldn't hear what the person was saying, even though I was listening as hard as I could.

"A'ite. Go to the spot and I'll be there," he said. With the phone call finished, he looked at me. "Baby, go to the trap house."

I didn't even ask what was going on again, I just drove and let *Thug Motivation* by Young Jeezy play.

When we reached the trap house on Wards Rd., it seemed like everyone was there. I took a seat by the table to the far right.

"Shit is crazy! Motherfuckers don't know who we are. They have consistently shown us that they don't respect our city or our hustle," Clap said, pacing the room.

Consistently? I thought to myself. *That could only mean...*

"Them Philly niggas that got bodied in the trailer court, their peoples is on a mission."

Yeah, I knew exactly what was going on, but how did they know that we were the ones who did that hit? Someone some place was talking, but who?

Ced looked at me and then at his crew.

"Those lame ass niggas is hungry for blood and I don't blame them 'cause if something happens to one of us, I'll be spillin' blood until there's none left," Ced was a dangerous man when he was angry.

I liked it. That nigga's mouth was making my pussy throb talking like that. There was no wonder why I loved him so much.

"Make sure y'all strapped at all times, no matter what. Even when y'all fuckin', make sure that strap is in reach," he told his crew.

Everyone acknowledged him with a nod of their head.

My mind was racing. Who the fuck was talking? I touched my side, comforted by the feel of my .45.

"Call around and see where these niggas at. I wanna know where they layin' their nappy ass heads. I want all the information," Ced barked his orders to his crew and walked out the door.

"These niggas can't break us. Let's show them what we're made of," I told them before I walked out the door.

Ced was in the car with his seat all the way pulled back. Once I was inside, I let him know exactly how I was feeling.

"Beauty is with Bella for a couple of days. Let's make it quick and clean them out."

"Sweets, you my fuckin' *rib,* girl."

Nothing else needed to be said. We both knew what was coming next.

By the time we got to the apartment on Old Forest Rd., his phone was jumping.

'Tonight it's goin' down, baby. Lynchburg is gonna have to get the Army, the Navy, and some more shit to find out what's goin' on."

"I wanna make sure of it," I told him, wiggling my fingers.

Jamaica

Chapter 11
Da Party's Over

It was 2:45 in the morning and every crew member was dressed in black from head to toe. Guns were being loaded while the city was sleeping.

"Four houses and eight niggas total," Ced informed his crew.

We'd gotten all the information in early that day. Every one of the crew members had put their ears to the streets and the streets talked back. Lynchburg welcomed no visitors, especially not ones that had a chance to make it out alive. I'd warned the Philly niggas when they'd first gotten there to leave but they refused to take orders from a bitch.

They'd brought boat to my city, fucked my income up a little, and turned my sperm donor into a boat smoked out junkie. So hell fucking yeah, they all had to pay, believe me they did, with their lives.

"If we don't make it back, let the city run nothin' but blood," Ced said.

"Don't speak for me, Ced," I told him straight up in front of his crew. I'd told that nigga plenty of times that I had a child that I wanted to raise.

His crew wasn't shocked. I hoped they all agreed with me.

"Let's get it then," he said with power in his voice.

So, it was me, Ced, Clap, and Trigger. Everyone else was chilling, unless we told them to move, and that was only if we had problems or didn't make it back. I was not worried. I always said, "I am comin' back."

First stop, 421 Walnut Street. I parked the Impala a block away from the house. Clap and Trigger were staying outside. Ced and I were going in. I checked my silencer to make sure it was on. I'd already put one in the head.

Nothing was covering my face because I was killing everything moving. All the lights were off in the house, and I liked it like that. Bam. Bam. Bam. I banged on the door with my back turned towards it.

"Sean, I know you in that motherfucker and you better let me in," I said loudly enough for someone inside to hear me.

Bam. Bam. Bam. I banged again.

"Who the fuck is it?" a male voice asked from the other side of the door.

"Sean open this fuckin'..."

The door swung open and everything happened fast. My .45 went off, two straight to the head. Ced moved in behind me as I crossed the threshold. He kicked the door closed and we both looked at the body on the floor. That nigga couldn't even be recognized. I hoped he had teeth and dental records.

I could smell weed and it was strong as hell, so strong it damn near covered the coppery smell of that nigga's blood all over the floor. I tilted my head, telling Ced to go that way, and he followed me into the bedroom ahead of us.

Drugs and alcohol were the death of those niggas. My next victim was literally hanging off the bed. He had emptied his stomach on the floor.

"Wake the fuck up, bitch," I told him, roughly poking the cold steel of my weapon against his head. He jerked away after the third poke and woke up a little confused, or just stupid, I couldn't tell.

"Huh? Who the fuck..."

I cut him off with a muffled pow, pow, pow, thanks to my silencer. His brains ended up in the puddle of vomit he'd left behind.

Ced smiled at me. I think he liked to watch me in action. I checked my watch and then I blew him a kiss. That job was finished in less than six minutes. Fuck with it. Those niggas had tried me. Now all I was gonna do was drop bodies and leave them looking like some chunky ass pasta sauce.

Second stop, Wise Street. An all-black Crown Vick was parked out front with the engine running. It looked like there were two people inside, too bad for them because I was on my way.

"Damn. These niggas must really, really want me dead, babe."

I could hear the worry in his voice, even though I couldn't see it on his face.

"I'm gonna murk these niggas. Have *no fear*, your babe is here." I blew him a kiss and showed him my .45.

He said, "These niggas don't know who the fuck we are."

Those niggas were on the go. I could see the nigga in the passenger seat. His legs were posted on the dash board, jiggling back and forth like he was impatient.

I took the lead and left Ced about twenty feet back. I knocked on the window with my left hand, and the nigga dropped his leg quickly. I could see his burner on his thigh in the light that was cast from the stereo display. The driver let the window down, like they were expecting somebody.

"How may I help you, beautiful?" that bitch ass nigga had the audacity to ask me.

"Help Me? Do I look like I need help?"

He must have felt the heat coming from my voice and my .45 was burning a hole through my black Dickies.

I saw the nigga's hand sliding towards the .9, but I was too fucking fast for his ass. Blocka. Blocka. Blocka. Straight head shots. The fucking driver couldn't have been strapped because he would have already pulled it.

Ced was standing by the driver's door, but the nigga was so focused on me and the brains in his lap that he didn't even see his own life ending.

Blocka. Blocka. Blocka.

There went my man getting his hands dirty again. He knew how it made me feel. *Tomorrow's news is gonna be ridiculous and I can't wait to watch it with my man. These pussy ass niggas tried taking him out. Ha-ha, that's not gonna happen on my watch.*

There were four down, and 4 left to go. I had some unfinished business to handle and I couldn't wait to get it done.

Warren Avenue at 3:20 in the morning was dark and quiet. Thanks to the Black G-Shock on my arm, I knew I had to hurry because the sun would be coming up soon.

"They say its 2104, a green house," Clap said from the front seat.

Trigger was driving, while me and Ced were in the back. I checked my glock to make sure I was ready to blast a nigga to eternity.

"Drop us off right here and circle the block. If we ain't out in four minutes, then come get our..."

"Ced, cut that shit out. I'll see y'all niggas in four minutes."

I hated when that nigga called death on my life. Damn. I knew that some people would say hope for the best and prepare for the worst, but fuck that. I'd say hope for the best and prepare for success.

When the car stopped, I welcomed the fresh air on my face. I took a deep breath and let it out slowly.

"You ready?"

"I am always ready. Let's finish these nigga's, baby," I told him in a sexy tone. I couldn't help it. Dropping bodies made my pussy wet.

A gray Toyota with Philly tags was parked in the driveway, so we knew we were at the right spot. That early in the morning, everyone was probably sleeping. That was good because I hated to leave nosey neighbors leaking, but that didn't mean I wouldn't.

The key that Trigger gave me worked. Some bitch he was fucking with knew the niggas, and he got her to make a copy of the key for him. I turned the lock with my left hand, but I had my glock in my right and it was ready to talk. I could feel Ced breathing on the back of my neck.

As I entered the house, all I could hear was snoring. It sounded like there was a bear in that mutha'fucka.

We took the long hallway on the right to where the noise was coming from. The door was halfway open, and I could see two bodies wrapped around each other. There was no need for lights because the street light was coming through the window perfectly, but I flipped the light on anyway. "Sleep is for the weak." Those Philly niggas disgusted me. Ced was standing in the doorway with his gun aimed at the bed. Them two niggas were gayed the fuck up.

"We'll give you whatever you want," the light skinned one said to us, blinking in the sudden light.

"You ain't got to give us shit. We brought something for you."

Ced and I fired in concert. We couldn't get any better at it if we practiced. That shit just came natural.

"They can fuck each other in hell," I said once we got back outside.

"That was only two minutes and fifty-six seconds, Sweets," Ced told me as he slapped my ass.

"Baby, we makin' records 'round here."

Our ride pulled up to where we were and we disappeared.

We were headed to the last stop of the mission and I was super crunk. I couldn't wait to be put to bed with some killa dick. I let Ced know how I was feeling by reaching over and lightly squeezing his dick with my right hand.

He looked into my eyes, just as hungry as I was.

"I got you, baby." I felt his breath on my ear as he whispered to me and his lips barely brushed my skin, sending goosebumps like wildfire from my neck to my feet.

Trigger pulled onto Shaffer Street and I suddenly had a feeling that this would be Twan and Telena's last night. I didn't want to pull up at 1625, so I closed my eyes and hoped I was wrong. I was not scared, I just was not ready to kill any children. I knew that was where they rested their heads also.

The Impala stopped and I relaxed just a little. When I opened my eyes, I saw that we were in front of a blue house that read 1629.

"1625 is the address," Trigger said over the back seat, and the momentary relief I'd felt at seeing 1629 disappeared.

I guess when your time comes, it's time for you to go, and only God can intervene.

"1625?" I asked, just wanting to make sure.

"Yea, you ready?" Ced asked.

"We all have to go in there. It's gonna be more than just two niggas," I informed them.

"How you know?" Trigger questioned me from the front seat.

"Cause I know, nigga," I snapped. He didn't have to know how I knew.

"Look, I'm gonna knock on the door. That's the best way in, 'cause all the lights are on in the house, meaning they probably in there smokin' and drinkin'. I know it's two Philly niggas that we're here for, but don't let anyone else live if they're in our way," I told them, looking at the house. My glock was loaded and ready to walk over anything moving.

As I approached the door, I could hear Young Joc's *New Joc City* album playing loudly. I tried the screen door, but it was locked, so I rang the bell and waited, hoping those niggas didn't shoot first and ask questions later.

The front door flew open.

"What's crackin', Sweets?" Twan asked, looking surprised.

My crew was standing against the house and listening to what we were saying. I knew they were ready to move. "I wanna talk to you, woman to man, on some real shit."

That was all it took. He unlocked the screen door that stood between the two of us, and just that quick, me, Clap, Trigger, and Ced were all up in that bitch.

Before the two niggas on the sofa could pull their guns, Clap and Trigger had their .45's in their faces.

"Where the kids at, Twan?" I asked him.

"They with their grandma." His voice was low.

"Where's that disloyal bitch of yours at?"

I had my joint all up in his face, ready to blast him right there and then.

"She went out with her friend."

Ced was searching the house to make sure that it was just the seven of us there.

"Coast clear, baby," he told me as he reached the bottom of the stairs.

"How the fuck you know these Philly niggas?" I asked, pushing Twan over to the sofa.

"Bitch, fuck you," the tall Sean Paul looking ass nigga said to me.

Pow. Pow. Pow.

The back of his head came off and splattered all over the nigga that were sitting beside him.

"Talk now, Twan," I told him. His whole body was stiff.

"Mane, Talena met this bitch and the bitch was like she knows where to get everything I need, so she hooked me up with them," he said, pointing towards his headless buddy on the bloody, brain juice covered sofa.

Ced jumped into the questioning. "Who's the bitch?"

"I don't even know her name, Cuz."

"Nigga, don't call me Cuz, we not family," Ced said as he stepped closer to Twan with anger in his eyes.

"Th... Th... The bitch's name is Dimples," he stuttered.

"Dimples? Describe her," I demanded.

"She white, she said y'all was cool, more like sisters. She said you the one that killed my brothers in the trailer."

I was mad as a wasp at that point and ready to sting because that nigga knew too much. And that bitch Dimples, I couldn't wait to get my hands on her.

"Smoke that nigga, Clap."

Immediately, he did the nigga the way I'd done Headless.

"Twan, I hope someone's prayin' for you."

Pow. Pow. Pow.

His body dropped from impact, and Ced jumped out the way.

When we got in the car, the clock on the dashboard said it was 4:01. It was time to see the rest of the crew. We'd been gone too damn long.

The drive was silent, but twenty minutes later we were at the trap house on Wards Road.

I knew for a fact that next time I would never leave anyone breathing. I learned from my mistakes. Leaving Dimples alive would haunt me until I crushed her.

"Have mercy on a real bitch, 'cause I am sinnin' every day, Lord. Have mercy on a real bitch, 'cause I'mma ride for my niggas, dawg," I said out loud. That was part of Ace Hood's song, but I felt like I was living it out.

"Amen," everybody else said in unison.

The crew was smiling and happy to see us all back. Those niggas were my family, right along with my daughter.

***

Midday news was about to come on any time and we were all staring at the 62-inch flat screen.

"I am Janet Saunders reporting today's midday news. A total of nine bodies have been discovered in various locations across the city. I am sending it over to Shawn, reporting live from 1625 Shaffer St."

The screen changed from the woman at a desk to a man on a sidewalk. He was in front of Twan's house.

"Thank you, Janet. Talena Holloway says that when she returned home this morning at 5am, she found a grisly scene. The father of her children and two of his friends had been slaughtered. No witnesses have come forward, and so far the police are closed mouthed about the investigation. The six other victims are all related. They arrived in Virginia a week ago from Philadelphia for a vacation, according to Ms. Holloway. The police are asking the city of Lynchburg to help them. Lead detective Thomas Johnson said earlier this morning that the four bodies that were found in the trailer on Lakeside Drive, and the seven bodies found today are all related. It seems the city of Lynchburg is a dangerous place to be. Back to you Janet."

"I told y'all them niggas didn't want any beef. Cut that shit off and let's get back to this money." Ced told his crew.

Jamaica

Chapter 12
Make a Wish

After a long day and night of love making between me and Ced, my body was aching in an extremely good way.

"Baby, I'm goin' to get Beauty. I need to show her some things."

Ced had a puzzled look on his face, and even with a puzzled expression, my man still looked sexy. Damn.

"What you got to show her that I can't see?"

"Just mother and daughter things, boo. She's seven years old and she needs to know how to handle herself when I ain't around."

"You can't be serious?"

"It's not what you think, Mr. Williams." I knew he loved it when I called him that.

"Corona, just make sure you don't regret what you're goin' to teach her."

"Believe me, I won't regret it, and neither will she."

I got out of bed and hit the shower so I could prepare myself for the day ahead of me. First, I needed to drop that hot ass rental at Enterprise. It was no good to me with nine bodies on it.

Hot water always relaxed me and put me in a great mood. I started rapping when the water hit my flesh.

"When I bang, I bang everythin' man,
Lift them off their feet,
Put them in a new van.
Wrap them in a box.
Jimmy Choo man!
I don't glamorize it,
I analyze it."

I called Beauty's grandma and she answered after only two rings.

"Bella, have Beauty ready for me. I'll be there in thirty minutes."

"Okay, Sweets."

I loved that woman. She was always ready.

I dropped the rental off and called a cab to take me to my own car. When I got there, it felt like eyes were watching me. Maybe I was paranoid, but Dimples was around and that made me nervous. I knew that bitch couldn't be slept on, especially when it came to me. I'd killed her parents and her lover, and I didn't give a fuck either.

That bitch Black was supposed to be my best friend, but naw, that bitch turned out to be my enemy and Dimples' lover.

When I arrived at Bella's house, Beauty was standing outside waiting for me with a smile on her face.

"Bella, thank you," I yelled to her out the window.

"Anytime, Sweets," she answered from the door. I knew that came from her heart and it made me feel blessed. I was glad my daughter had her.

Beauty sat in the front seat and turned the system up, bobbing her head to the beat. Lil Boosie's song *I'm Mad* was jumping through the speakers, but I turned the music down so I could talk to my baby girl while I drove.

"Beauty, what do you want to be when you grow up?" My eyes were on the road, but I could see her just right.

"Ma, you want the truth?"

"Yes, I want the truth and nothin' but the truth," I told her firmly. I'd rather have the truth than a lie. I wanted our relationship to be unbreakable, something that *nothing* and *no one* could *destroy*.

"I want to be just like you." She'd told me that before, but I wanted to make sure that she was sure.

I knew she was only seven, but I wanted her to understand that her word was all she had.

"Ma, I want to be just like you," she said again.

That was all I needed to hear because that day she'd get the lesson that would change her life forever.

Candles Mountain Rd was our first stop. I turned the music back up and let *I'm Mad* keep bumping.

All kinds of thoughts were running through my head, and I let them run their course. My mind was already made up. I'd rather teach Beauty sooner than later. Train a child in the way you want them to grow so when they get older they will not depart from it.

"Grab the bag from the back seat," I told her when we parked.

We were in the mountains, all the way up *in* the mountains, no houses in sight, only trees.

"You ready, boo?" I asked looking into her pretty face.

"Ma, I am always ready." That girl was mine through and through and she proved it every time she opened her mouth.

"What I'm about to show you, you have to promise me that you won't tell anyone. This is our little secret."

"Loyalty is a MUST, mom, and we're bonded by blood," she answered solemnly.

I was proud to call her my child, and knowing that my blood was running through her veins was the best gift I'd *ever* received. I knew she'd always make me proud.

I removed my .9 from the waist of my jeans and showed it to her. "This is one of my best friends," I told her.

Her face was unreadable, just like a poker player, and I was loving it.

I put a bullet in the head by cocking it back, then I put my finger on the trigger and pulled that back too.

Pow. The sound echoed through the trees.

Beauty didn't even jump. Her eyes were glued to the gun. I put the .9 down and opened the bag that I'd taken from the car.

"This one is yours," I told her as I showed her the baby .22.

"For real?" I heard excitement in her voice.

"Every time you're with me, it's yours."

"You gonna let me shoot it, Ma?"

Damn, she was ready already. That was my girl.

"You think you can handle it?" I asked her just to hear her answer.

"You're gonna show me how to handle it, right?"

"Of course," I assure her, it was my pleasure.

We spent two hours in the mountains having our mother and daughter time.

"Remember what I asked you earlier?" I asked her when we were on our way home.

"Yea. And my answer was, I want to be just like you."

"And just like your mother you will be." Even if I died that day, I would've died with a happy face because my baby was ready to go.

"Remember, you can't tell anyone," I reminded her.

"Mom, you told me once, you don't have to tell me twice. It's our secret forever."

Chapter 13
Read Between the Lines

I was going to attend Twan's funeral, and I'd decided to take Beauty with me.

"You're crazy for goin', and a maniac for takin' Beauty," Ced told me before I left the house, but he let me go.

Death was real and it was serious, which made it *real serious*. She needed to see it for herself.

I was surprised the church was so packed. I could see Talena and her family in the front row. A woman to the left with a big ugly hat was screaming, "Why, Lord, why?" even though the pastor was talking.

"As parents, we feel that we should be buried by our children. We never feel that we should be the ones to bury them, but God calls whom he calls. We teach them at a young age to love thy neighbor and do the right things, but they change as they get older and end up doing their own things. When we live by the world, we die by the world. The heart of this world is too cold, which is why we need to live in the *Word* of the Lord."

I heard him. What the pastor was saying made sense, but I'd given Twan enough time to make it right with God, so that was on him.

"As we close, I pray that if you don't know the Savior, that you will get to know him."

A white lady behind Talena was rubbing on her shoulders, while the lady to the left continued crying, "Why?"

We were seated at the back of the church, in the last row, but I had a pretty good view from where we sat and we were close to the door. The white lady got up, and I was shocked.

"Ma, that's Auntie Dimples," I heard Beauty's voice loud and clear.

My eyes locked with hers from across the room. She knew what time it was. Her feet stopped and my right hand was on my hip. I stayed strapped, and she knew that too.

"Read between the lines," I mouthed to her.

She turned around and headed back to her seat behind Talena.

"It's time to go, Beauty," I said, pulling her in front of me to keep my body between my daughter and my enemy as we exited the First Baptist Church of God on 16th Street.

That bitch knew that I knew she'd told them Philly niggas all about me. I wondered how she felt, knowing that they all died because they listened to her ass.

"Mom, why didn't you say anything to Auntie Dimples?" Beauty wanted to know as soon as we pulled away from the church.

"Now is the time to tell her everything," the little red devil on my left shoulder whispered in my ear.

"Don't make her heart cold. She's only a child," the white angel on the opposite side shouted into my other ear.

I looked at my child and I knew I had to keep it real with her. Those bitches on my shoulders were gonna argue no matter what. "Beauty, do you know the meaning off the word *real*?"

"I think I do." Her voice was solid.

"Tell me what you think it means."

"It means that you are not fake. Santa Clause is fake, he doesn't bring any gifts. Your money is real 'cause it buys all my presents."

That was the best example ever.

"Well, baby, what I am about to tell you is real, so please listen and pay attention."

For the next few hours, I told Beauty everything and I mean *everything*. I told her when I met Dimples and Black, how they turned on me, even how I killed Black, and let Dimples live because she'd had a hard life.

Beauty showed no emotions as I spoke and laid out the ugly truth of things. She just listened, and not once did she ask me any questions.

"Beauty, I trust no one, 'cause no one can be *trusted.* You are my child and I trust you, but I want you to keep your heart cold and your mind open at all times.

"Ma, all you have to do is teach me, and I promise you, I will *never* let you down."

I took my eyes off the road to look at my child, and I knew that was me right there, a little version of Sweets.

I was so *proud.*

Jamaica

Chapter 14
Show Me You're Ready
Two weeks later…

Since Twan's murder, it seemed that Jay was *the man*. Not that it surprised me, because he was a boss in his own way. But living in Lynchburg, there will be only one *boss* and one *boss bitch*, which were Ced and myself.

Traymon was smoking himself to death, and he didn't even look the same anymore. His appearance was awful, he smelled terrible, and he was always high on that fucking *boat*.

"Nigga, boat is killin' you. All you wanna do is sit around here and get high," I yelled at him after I found him on the block while I was looking for Jay.

"Life is fu-fu-fucked up," he told me. The nigga couldn't even talk.

I put him in my car and drove his ass to his house. When I pulled up, Regina was outside talking to some ol' lady.

"Help me bring this nigga in the house," I yelled to her.

She literally ran to the car. We carried him into the house and put him on the sofa.

"Life, life is fucked up," he said again. I was sick of that shit.

"I'll be back at 3:30," I snapped at her and left. I was so mad at that nigga.

*****

"Beauty, you have to tell your father to change his ways."

Tears immediately filled her eyes. Her father did no wrong as far as she was concerned.

"Ma, I know he gets high. He is high all the time. The way he looks at me like I have two heads, he stutters all the time, and it takes him forever to get to the kitchen from the living room, plus whatever he smokes stinks."

Beauty was crying by the time she finished her statement, and seeing her like that broke my heart. It made me wanna smoke Traymon's ass, but I knew she'd never forgive me if I did.

"Look at me," I gently said to her.

When she lifted her head, I noticed how long her hair was getting. It was braided up and kicked to a side pony. She was gonna be too grown too soon and all I could do was get her ready for the things no one had gotten me ready for.

"You gonna have to make him choose, either stop smokin' or leave your life alone."

I knew that was harsh, but she had to do that. It could save both of them so much heartache. Maybe he'd straighten up to be around his daughter and help me raise her, not that I needed him to, but for her sake.

It was after 3pm when we pulled up in front of T's house. I parked at the curb in front of the house. Regina was still outside talking to the same ol' lady from earlier.

"He still inside?" I asked her as Beauty and I headed for the door.

"Yea, he's in there."

Traymon was in the same place I'd left him, still looking and smelling fucked up.

"Yo, I brought Beauty to see you," I told him.

"Come gi-give da-dada a kiss."

His fucking voice was getting on my nerves already. I watched quietly as my little girl walked over to him and stopped.

"Daddy, you and mommy made me, so that means y'all's blood is running through me. Right now you're weak, and I don't need to be around that. I want to be a leader. I don't want to be like you. My blood is too strong for me to be weak. If you need help, mommy will get you help, but if you don't, I don't ever want to come over here again."

My daughter spoke those words carefully, as if she'd thought about them for a long time. Maybe she had. That child of mine was something else.

Traymon was immediately ashamed, and he broke eye contact to drop his head. Beauty's face was serious as the grave.

"If you want help, open the door when we leave. If you don't open the door, then I'll know you don't want to be my daddy anymore. Ma, let's go," she said like she was running shit. She didn't even look back as she walked toward the door.

Well, damn. I was at a loss for words. I saw my child hurting and it killed me. But she was handling it like a *boss*. I couldn't help but be *proud* of her.

"You better get your shit right, nigga," I told T before I followed Beauty.

She walked past Regina and the ol' lady without even acknowledging them. My baby girl knew the meaning of *real* and she was living it.

We got in the car and waited to see what Traymon did. I was going to give that nigga sixty seconds to open that door, and if he didn't, I was going to kill his ass. My mind was made up.

"Never let anyone see your emotions, baby. They'll take advantage of you when you're down."

Forty seconds left...

"It's okay to cry, but cry in the shower. Cryin' is good for the soul, but it will also show others what hurts you. Don't think I don't cry."

Twenty seconds left...

"Mommy cries inside," I told her as I touched my heart. I knew this was hard for her, especially at her age.

"But cryin' in public or around other people is somethin' I will *not do*."

Six seconds left...

"You protect your heart from everyone."

The door flew open as soon as I finished my sentence. The smile that appeared on my daughter's face was priceless.

"We gonna get daddy help, Boo," I tell her as we pulled away from the crib.

I called the Men's Rehab center on Main Street to see if they had a space for Traymon. The receptionist said there was a bed open, so I gave her Traymon's info and told her I'd be there to drop him off in two hours.

Regina packed Traymon's bags, and Beauty took them to the car. I could tell he was finally coming down because his movements were faster and the stuttering was gone."

"Yo, I'ma get my shit together," he told me, not that I cared. I cared about Beauty and she was the only reason why I was doing that. She deserved a good father.

"I love you, baby girl," he told Beauty as he stepped out of the car when we arrived at the center.

It was going to cost twelve hundred dollars for thirty days. I hoped the shit worked or his ass was gonna be dead, by my hand.

"I love you too daddy!"

I knew that shit was gonna make him better. Not being able to see Regina was gonna be hard for him, but I hoped he did it for his child.

He had to.

"Damn," I said out loud, wondering how he could let drugs get the best of him.

We watched him enter the building before we pulled off.

"Beauty, it's gonna be okay." I could see the worry all over her pretty face.

Every day while Beauty was at school, I called to see how Traymon was doing, and so far every report had been better than the last. I hoped he kept it together. If the nigga was smart, Beauty would be his glue. If he was not, I'd be his *end*.

Chapter 15
I am Coming

It had been weeks since I'd seen Jay or heard anything about him. It was time to do something about that lack of info.

After I put Beauty to bed for the night, I dressed myself in all black.

"You don't give up, do you?" Ced asked me on my way out the door.

"*Never.*"

Since I couldn't find Jay, I thought I'd just drop everyone around him until he showed up, because he *would* show up.

De'Bonye lived on Lindsay Street, so that was exactly where I was heading. That bitch lived with her grandparents, which was good because they'd find her body quickly.

I parked the rental that Ced had gotten for me at the end of the block and walked the rest of the way to 731. I had my hoodie pulled up, my leather gloves on, and my silencer already attached to my .9. I was going to do this shit face to face. It was 1:45 in the morning. I hoped her grandparents were asleep, not that I discriminated, because anyone could and would get it if they were in my way. That was just the way it was.

I knocked lightly on the door and turned my face towards the street. Ten seconds passed before I knocked a little louder.

"Who is it?" a voice behind the door asked me, but I didn't answer.

I was waiting for the door to open. When it did, I turned around to see who it was. Exactly who I went there for. She didn't recognize me because I had black chalk all over my face.

She tried to run, but I was faster than her. I plunged my gun dead in her mouth as I grabbed her and used my left hand to pull her towards me. I could smell the fear on her.

"Bitch, you tell Jay to come find me," I told her ass.

I let two shots off. Her head exploded all over the wall, and I could feel her blood soaking through my shirt. I held onto her body so it wouldn't wake anyone up when it hit the floor. I laid her down softly and closed the door before I walked away like I hadn't just taken a life.

"That bitch ain't had shit on her mind," I said out loud while I smelled my .9 when I entered the rental.

Ced was fast asleep when I returned home, and when I checked, so was Beauty. I grabbed a trash bag from the kitchen and headed towards the shower. I had to get that bitch off of me.

I took my clothes off and placed them piece by piece into the bag. Then I got in the shower.

I was back and ready to watch motherfuckers go crazy. Jay was probably out with Regina when he should've been at home with his so-called seed.

I took my time in the shower, but when I finished, it was back to business. I took the bag with my clothes in it and hit the back yard. Once I was there, I doused it with fuel and lit it up. Then I stuck around to watch it burn.

"Glad to see you up." Ced came out of nowhere. I didn't even hear him until he spoke.

"You know me."

He gave me a long look and left me there to watch the flames alone, which was cool with me because I would've rather it be that way.

After twenty or thirty minutes, I was left with nothing but ashes. It was Saturday, so I'd probably be sleeping in and getting me some much needed rest. Ced was once again fast asleep when I enter the bedroom. I crawled up under the blanket and lay my head on his chest. He stirred a little and wrapped his left arm around me. Off to sleep I went.

"Sweets, you doin' too much. You teachin' Beauty how to be cold just like you, and you don't need to be doin' that. Once she turns cold, there ain't no turnin' back. No one will be able to change her, not even herself."

I found myself looking into my brother's face as if he'd never died.

"I'm doin' the right thing, King. I want her to be colder than me so *no* one will be able to hurt her. Remember, you was the same one who told me to turn my heart cold to protect myself. I'm mad at you for tellin' me how to raise my child."

"You see how you are now? Well, Beauty will be *unstoppable*."

"And that's exactly how I want her to be, *un-fuckin'-stoppable*."

I woke up alert, like I was never even asleep.

Damn, that was a crazy ass dream, I thought to myself as I sat up in the bed. I looked at Ced and he was staring at the T.V. When he saw I was awake, he turned the volume up so I could hear. The alarm clock told me it was only 7:30.

"Early this morning, officers were called to 731 Lindsay Street. Upon arrival, they found a young black female shot to death at her own front door. She is survived by a young child and her grandparents, who refuse to comment. The name of the victim has yet to be released to the media. Merrick will have more details at noon."

I dropped back in the bed and pulled the soft blanket up over my head, thinking about the dream that I'd had of my brother. I felt a sudden pang of loss. Damn, I missed King. I knew Ced was just lying there looking at me, but I didn't care. "Rest in peace, King," I said out loud, knowing it must've sounded crazy to him, but I didn't care about that either. Then my mind ran in the other direction.

Jay wanted to play games. Well, I was the wrong one to be playing with. He was gonna fuck around and have *everybody* dead because his ass wanted to hide.

I heard Ced's phone ringing, so I pulled the blanket from over my face so I could see and hear him better.

"Yo'," he answered, looking at me.

"I just seen it on the news, Steven."

Ced was talking to his father.

"So how's he takin' it?" Ced asked.

He put it on speakerphone so I could hear both sides of the conversation.

"Well, you know, he had just got the blood test back sayin' that's his baby."

Was I hearing things? Damn, I'd just killed Jay's babyma. A smile appeared on my face. Now I knew that I'd hit him where it was gonna hurt for real.

I got out of bed and left the room. Ced's mouth was hanging wide open, just how I wanted it to be. He'd better tell his brother to turn himself in to me because the bodies I was planning on dropping were the bodies he loved.

Chapter 16
So Many Surprises

Beauty was up and brushing her teeth.

"Good morning, Sleeping Beauty," I said to her, kissing the top of her head.

She pulled the toothbrush from her mouth to answer me. "Morning, Mom. I had a bad dream last night."

"What was it about, baby?" I asked her as she spit in the sink.

"It was about daddy."

I couldn't read her face, but I wished I could. She rinsed her mouth out and laid her toothbrush on the counter. "What about your daddy, Beauty?"

"Somebody killed him and we buried him, Mom."

Her face seemed to drop with sadness. But what could I do if her dream did come true? Nothing. Everyone had a day coming. It didn't matter who they were. If it was their time to go, then they were gone.

I forced myself to ask her the unthinkable, "How would you feel if somethin' was to happen to your father?"

She looked me dead in the eye and said, "Whoever hurts him, I would like to hurt them back ten times worse, all by myself." The love she had for T was above and beyond anything I'd ever felt for my own father. I wished I'd had even a tenth of that for my dad, but killing him only made me better, *stronger*.

"Let's just hope your Daddy makes you proud," I told her as I watched her carefully. She walked away and left me standing in her bathroom.

It was as good a time as any to check on T. I dialed the Rehab Center to see how he was doing. "Hello. I am calling regarding Mr. Traymon Davis," I said when they picked up.

I listened to the receptionist with a sinking feeling in my gut, and shook my head.

"Thank you for your time," I told her before I hung the phone up.

After only fifteen fuckin' days, that boat-head motherfuckin' nigga checked himself out. Not only did my fuckin' money go down the drain, but this was gonna break Beauty's little heart.

I could hear the shower running as I passed our bedroom. Ced must've been getting himself together.

Beauty was in the kitchen making herself some cereal, Captain Crunch. I took a seat at the table and watched her.

"Mom, would you like me to make you a bowl?"

"No, thank you." I closed my eyes for a minute, because I had to tell her exactly what I'd just found out about her father. As I opened up my eyes, she was seated across from me, head deep in her cereal bowl.

"Ma, are you okay?"

My face always gave me away when it came to her.

"I am okay, but you probably won't be."

She stopped eating immediately and stared at me. Her poker face was always on, so I continued.

"Your father left the Center."

She released the spoon from her hand, and it fell into the bowl splashing milk onto the table.

"Beauty, we tried to help him, but he's either not ready to change, or maybe he's already changed." I had to put that in there to give her some hope. I couldn't bear to crush her completely. Besides, what if it was true?

A smile spread across her face, and she picked her spoon up as she looked at me.

"I think that little time changed him." She dipped her spoon into her bowl, brought it to her mouth, and smiled at me. For her to be seven going on eight she was a very strong little lady.

"Good morning, Dad."

I turned around to find Ced behind me. I was not surprised by his silence, but I knew I'd just heard Beauty call him "Dad." I looked at him and then back at her. She was once again head deep in the bowl. I looked back at my man and winked.

"Good morning, princess," he said as he walked past me to kiss Beauty on her forehead.

"Good morning, my Queen," he sang to me as he opened up the fridge.

He could make me smile so easily. "Good morning, my King," I replied. We were a royal family. "What you have planned for today?" I asked as he grabbed a Redbull.

"On my way to get the kids so we can spend some family time together."

"I can't wait to see my brother and sisters," Beauty squealed with excitement. She jumped down from her chair and ran from the kitchen, leaving the empty bowl on the table after slurping the milk down.

Ced's facial expression was priceless, and I could tell how happy he was. So was I. I couldn't help but wonder what the hell was going on in that little head of my daughter's, and I knew Ced was thinking the very same thing.

"I'll be back in about forty minutes," he told me as he kissed my lips.

"Your Queen will be here waiting."

I watched him leave the kitchen and I listened for the front door to close. Then I picked up Beauty's bowl and put it in the sink.

"Ma, your phone's up here ringin'," she screamed down to me from upstairs.

"Okay." I made it up the stairs, but not in time to catch the call. The caller had hung up.

"434-873-2928, who the fuck is that?" I asked out loud.

I called the number back as I got myself ready for the shower.

"Yo," a male voice answered.

"Who dis?"

"Babyma, it is me, nigga." Damn, the nigga even sounded different.

"What's up with you?" I asked him.

"Shit, just chilling, missing you and our baby girl." For some reason, he sounded like he was telling me the truth.

"How was your vacation?"

"Mane, that shit was all I needed, but I just couldn't stay there no damn thirty fuckin' days yo."

Beauty walked into my room and jump on my bed.

"As long as it helped you, that's all that matters."

Beauty's eyes were glued to the flat screen, but I knew her ears were in my phone conversation.

"I just wanna tell you thank you so much for doin' that for me. A nigga was in the dark, and you was my passage to light. You have always been a real ass bitch to me, no matter what I've put you through."

"And I'm always gonna to be a real bitch, *always*."

Beauty's toes were wiggling.

"You want to talk to your little lady?"

"You know I do."

I handed Beauty the phone and waited for her face to light up when she heard her father's voice.

"Daddy, I miss you so much. Are you better?"

The smile that appeared on her face was invaluable. I took my ass to the shower to give her some space so she could catch up with her father.

So far it was looking to be an amazing day. I was thrilled that nigga had gotten his shit together because the hurt he was causing my princess was heartbreaking.

I reflected on my year, and all the things that had happened while I let the hot water beat on my back. I had to say how grateful I was to be alive, but I wanted Jay to know that I was coming for him. *And I would never stop.*

Jamaica

Chapter 17
Yup, T Did It

Beauty was still talking to T, and she was still posted up in my bed when I got out of the shower.

"A'ite, Daddy. I love you and miss you. Stay out of trouble and do the right thing."

I was getting dressed, but I was listening to her talk, too. I guess she got that from me.

"Ma, Daddy says store his number and hit him up later," she relayed to me.

"Tell him okay."

"A'ite, Daddy. I'm gone," she told him and ended the call.

"Beauty. Beauty." Suddenly we heard Cobra screaming Beauty's name like she was lost in a jungle someplace.

Beauty took off out of my bed in a rush, screaming back. "Here I am."

Ced was back with the kids. Even though I expected him, I still didn't hear him coming, but there was no mistaking the feel of his hands on my lower back. "Don't try me," I told him while I looked for something easy to put on.

"Why try you, when I can get it any time?" he responded.

"The kids are here," I reminded him.

"So what?"

"I wanna enjoy you, so let's play later," I said, turning to face him.

The Fruit of the Loom wife beater I was wearing was hugging me perfectly and I knew it. I kissed his lips and walked off, leaving him there looking at me. Sometimes easy was sexy.

"I'mma have you pay for that later on tonight," he told me.

So I punished him even more. I bent over, revealing my ass to him from the back, and then replied, "Don't think for a second that I wouldn't love it either."

I could hear the kids running up the stairs, and it sounded like they were coming to the room, so I grabbed Ced's blue and white Polo shorts from the edge of the bed and pulled them on quickly.

"Sweets," Christina yelled as she ran towards me with her arms wide open.

"Hey, baby," I welcomed her into my arms. She looked more like her father the older she got.

"Sweets, I missed you too," Ced Jr. told me as he jumped on the bed. He was Ced himself.

Lord, please help these young ladies growing up, 'cause this one is gonna have more than one lady in his life, I silently prayed. Next thing I knew, Ced Jr., Beauty, Cobra, and Christina were all jumping up and down in my bed.

I grabbed Lil Miss Cobra and asked her, "So you don't miss me?"

"You know I do, Sweets, but I missed Beauty more." She kissed my cheek and flashed a pretty smile at me.

Beauty and Cobra were attached at the hip. Blood couldn't have made them any closer, and I loved it.

Ced was just standing by the wall looking at us. He was so happy to see us together, and it showed all over his face.

"I'm goin' to my room to play the PS3," Ced Jr. said as he jumped from the bed and headed out of the room.

"So am I. Well, not really. I'm gonna get on the computer," Christina said with a laugh. We all laughed at her because we knew she was addicted to Instagram.

"Me and Beauty gonna go chill in our room," Cobra grabbed her newest sister by the hand and they left the room running.

Ced was looking at me like he was hungry. Even though I already knew what he wanted to eat, I asked him anyway. "Are you hungry?"

"Do you plan on feedin' me some of this?" He slid his hand between my legs and grabbed my pussy.

106

"Later, Big Daddy." Once again, I left him standing there. I knew I was gonna be punished later, and I was moist just thinking about it.

The kids were scattered throughout the house, and Ced was sitting at the table on his phone while I was getting dinner ready.

"I gotta fuck that joint real quick, 'cause that other bitch is gone."

I knew what I was hearing, so I looked at him and he smiled at me.

"I'm chillin', so on Monday mornin' we gonna smash the bitch while the kids at school."

The only bitch that he would be smashing was that pure white cocaine.

"A'ite, Fam, say hello to wifey for me, too." He laughed before he spoke again. "Oh yea, she standin' here lookin' at me all crazy and shit. Her brain's doin' jumpin' jacks."

I threw the tomato I was holding at him, but he caught it in his left hand. Damn, that nigga was quick. Quick + Quiet = Deadly. I loved it.

"A'ite, Fam," he said and hung up the phone.

"Your ass is all up in my conversation." He tossed the tomato back to me. I snatched it out of the air. Shit, I was quick too.

"Next time, don't talk around me then." We both laughed, but his phone rang and disrupted our laughter.

"Yo." He set his phone down and hit the speaker button.

"I know you listenin', but listen' good and please understand what I am 'bout to say."

"Nigga, I know you ain't callin' my phone…"

I cut Ced off to put in my own two cents. "Let him speak."

"You want problems? 'Cause I know you did it, Sweets."

Am I trippin'? I know I didn't hear pain in Jay's voice. Let me find out this nigga done turned soft over a bitch, I thought.

"Look, I really don't appreciate you callin' my man's phone lookin' for me, and then havin' the nerve to try goin' ham on me. Do me…"

"Bitch, fuck you. I'mma finish your ass when I see you again," Jay screamed.

I could tell Ced was fuming over Jay's arrogance. His face was suddenly hard and it looked like it had been carved out of stone.

"I ain't never run from a nigga and I damn sure ain't 'bout to start now, so fuck you," I said my piece and hung the phone up.

I understood that Ced was between a rock and a hard place, but I knew he better not cross over on me.

"Don't let that shit fuck your day up, baby. I am not lettin' it get to me," I told him, meaning every word I said. *Fuck that nigga Jay. He wanna talk shit, I was gonna let him eat that shit.*

Ced was pissed off, and I had to find a way to cheer him up. Jay wasn't gonna ruin my day.

"You still want this Kitty for dinner?" I put his left hand between my legs on that kitty cat he liked so much, and a smile appeared on his face. Maybe he remembered I was supposed to be punished.

"You know I do."

"Let's finish this day so tonight will be beautiful." I winked at him, and then walked away.

The tension in the room wasn't all the way gone but it was not that strong anymore. Jay didn't want no problems with me.

"I'm gonna check up on the kids," Ced stated and smacked my ass as he walked past me.

That shit Jay was talking was *all* shit, because after I put Ced to sleep, I was gonna show him who the real bitch was.

Dinner was off the hook. We had baked chicken breasts, fried rice, mac-n-cheese, and collard greens. We all sat at the table and ate family style. When we finished, we played a few board games, and around nine, the children hit the shower. By eleven, they were all fast asleep.

Ced helped me clean the kitchen and living room up.

"Now it's our time," I whispered in his ear.

"Let me punish you then."

I led the way to our room. As soon as he closed the door, I let my clothes hit the floor and walked naked to the shower.

"D-a-a-m-m-n," he said as he rubbed his hands together.

As I hit the shower, I saw him coming into the bathroom behind me. "Let me wash you clean," he told me.

"Can I do the same?"

"We belong to each other always and forever."

He washed my body from my hair to my feet and I did the same for him. Once we were done, he carried me to the bed with our bodies still dripping water.

"I love you, Corona."

He better had. "I love you too, Ced."

Our lips met and my body replied the only way it should have when it came to him, I got *wetter.* He let me fall onto the bed as he sucked my nipples one at a time. I threw my head back in pleasure because I knew this was going to be great.

"Tell me how you want me to please you, Sweets."

"Do as you please, Ced, I belong to you."

"Always?"

"And forever, Mr. Williams."

He kissed the scar on my chest, next my stomach, and then he put his tongue inside my navel. He worked his way down to my pussy. I looked down between my thighs at him, and as his tongue touched my pearl, I dropped my head back on the pillow again. He was a master at eating my pussy. He used his hands to put my legs up on his shoulders, and without pausing he found my arms and placed both of my hands on the back of his head.

"Oh my," I gasped. My legs were doing the Crip dance on his back, and I knew I was about to cum all in his mouth. The more I arched my back, the better I felt his tongue, and my nut was so damn close.

"Cum for daddy," he told me.

I did as he said and came all in his mouth.

After eating up all my juices, he kissed my clit and said, "How sweet, now I have a sweet tooth."

"Let me show you how to punish someone properly," I told him pulling him up from between my legs.

I saw that smirk on his face and I knew he thought he was ready for me, but I planned on showing him how a real punishment was supposed to be. He stood up from the edge of the bed, and I eased my way down between his legs. He was rock solid and I could see all his veins. If having a pretty dick was a crime, he would've gotten life in prison because his joint was beautiful.

I gently placed the tip of my tongue on the head of his dick. I gazed up at him to watch his reaction. He was smiling down on me, and I loved his smile. I circled my tongue around the tip as I let it slide into my warm, wet mouth. I placed my right hand onto his dick as I used my left hand to play with his balls. I sucked him up and down as I stroked him.

A groan of pleasure escaped from his mouth. He tried to use his hand to guide my head, so I released his balls from my left hand and moved his hand from my head. I let his dick slip out of my mouth.

"Don't touch me," I commanded him.

The look he gave me told me to do me, and that's exactly what I planned on doing.

I ran my tongue all the way down his dick until my lips were on his balls. I sucked them slowly as I beat his dick fast. He was looking down on me, wanting to touch me, but he knew he had to play by my rules. I used my left hand to open his legs wider. I licked under his balls before placing them both in my mouth at the same damn time while I beat him off with my hand.

"Damn. What the fuck you doin' to me?" he gasped.

I didn't respond since my mouth was full, but I decided to go in for the kill. I blew cold air from my mouth onto his dick and then I put it back in my mouth. I used both hands to hold his ass so he could fuck my mouth like never before. I could feel his legs shaking and I knew any minute that I'd be drinking my vitamin A, B, C, *and* D, and I was ready to swallow it all.

"Let, me taste you," I told him.

And he did exactly what I said. He grabbed the back of my head with both of his hands and exploded down my throat. I drank every bit of it. Nothing needed to be left behind, so I cleaned him up with my mouth.

When I was done, I told him, "You taste great, Daddy."

He gave me that beautiful smile again. "You really know how to punish a nigga fa' real."

I smiled at him as I climbed into the bed. "Now come and finish me."

For two hours, we pleased and enjoyed each other's bodies from head to toe.

I was hurting from all that fucking, but I was still ready to show Jay a thing or two. The alarm clock showed 1:45am. Ced was fast asleep on his stomach. I removed myself quietly from the bed so I could get dressed and handle my business.

Jamaica

Chapter 18
Bitch

It was time for that all *black*. I was in the basement lacing up my Timberlands when I saw a shadow fall in front of me, and even though I didn't hear shit, I knew it was Ced. Or maybe it was *because* I didn't hear shit that I knew it was him. He moved like a ghost. I never heard his feet.

"I know what you have to do, and I know I can't stop you, but please promise me you're comin' back."

I didn't even look up to see his face because his voice was enough. I continued to lace my Timbs.

"I'm the *queen* of this mansion, and it can't be run without *me*," I answered.

"I'll be waitin' for you, My Queen."

I still didn't look up, and he didn't make me. He just gave me the space I needed to do what had to be done.

I knew it was hard for him to see me leave, not knowing what was going to happen, but he needed to have faith in me. I'd never let him down before, and I didn't plan to. I was coming back for my family and that was a *fact*.

I was ready to go. I checked my best friend, my .9, to make sure everything was straight, and I left the house by the back door to avoid going through the rest of the house.

Ced had a grey Toyota Camry that he hardly ever drove, so I was going to borrow it for my own purpose.

I put in Young Jeezy's CD *The Inspiration* to motivate me, and I put it on my favorite track *The Realest* as I drove away from everyone I loved. I let his words speak to me like never before.

"You know the feelin',
Your heart fall to your feet.
Summer time niggas,
Still ridin' with the heat."

***

Time flew when I was on a mission, especially a mission that I was so determined to accomplish. Jay's mother lived on Sussex Street, and that was where I was going. It was nothing against her. It was all about her son's actions. I was doing this for Ced's mother, also. She could really rest in peace, knowing that the woman her true love cheated with was going to finally pay.

I parked the car at the end of the block, but I left the keys in the ignition because it was only gonna take a minute.

As I walked the block, I couldn't hear anything, no birds, no cats, or even dogs were out. Everything and everyone was sleeping and that was how I liked it.

As I approached the house, I could see the lights were on. It had been a long time since I'd been there, but my memory was good, and I could tell exactly which rooms were lit up. There were lights on in the bathroom, kitchen, and the living room.

Maybe someone was awake.

I climbed the steps on the porch to make my way to the front door. The curtains were so thin I could see right into the living room. Pictures of Jay and his sisters were all over the walls. Towards the left of the room, I could see a body on the sofa, and with the good luck that I was having, it was his mother lying there. She looked like she was asleep. I watched her chest rise and fall for a second before I cracked the window with the butt of my gun.

The sound it made woke her, and she sat up straight, looking dead at me. My trigger finger was faster than her mouth. She didn't have time to say shit. I let two shots off into her head, and it opened up like an over ripe melon.

As quickly as I came, I left.

If Jay didn't want to turn himself in, then being the *bitch* that I was, I was going to *kill* everything that he loved, *no questions asked.*

Jamaica

Chapter 19
Just Like Me

The entire house was sleeping, except for Beauty, when I got home. She was sitting in the living room watching reruns of *The Cosby Show* with a can of Pepsi in her lap. I was kind of surprised to see her up so late by herself.

"Why are you up, baby?"

Her eyes were still focused on the screen, but her right hand was tucked under her leg.

"I couldn't sleep, so I went to your room to get you up, but you wasn't there, so I grabbed the best friend that you gave me and came downstairs to wait on you."

She focused her eyes dead at me as she removed the .22 out from under her leg and showed it to me. The light from the T.V. glinted off the shiny silver of the brand new weapon.

"Why are you dressed all in black?" she cross-examined me.

"I had to handle some business," I told her, looking into her eyes.

The look on her face showed me that she wanted to know more about my business, so I took a seat beside her, and she shifted her eyes back to the T.V screen.

"I know you remember Jay."

When she bobbed her head up and down, I continued, "Well, he shot me. That's why I was in the hospital. He tried to kill me."

Her face dropped and she closed her eyes for a second before looking at me with a devilish smile.

"He tried to kill you, Ma? Please tell me you gonna make him pay?" she sounded just as excited as when she talked about candy.

"I've started already, and I don't want you to worry about me 'cause I'm gonna get him." My voice was low, but loud enough for her to hear me. I was hoping no one else was up.

"If you need me in anyway, let me know. I am your child," she told me. She got up from the couch, kissed my forehead and left the room, with her .22 still in her hand.

There I was worrying about having someone to watch my back, when all along my child was willing to ride with me and for me.

That nigga had me up and losing sleep, but I'd rather have lost sleep than my life. Fucking with me, he no longer had his mom, or his babyma. Soon, and *very* soon, his ass was gonna be grass because I was going to put him in the ground.

I turned the flat screen off and headed upstairs. I could hear slow music playing in my room on the sound system, but Ced was fast asleep. I stripped down and carried my ass to the shower to get fresh so I could wrap up with my man.

As the hot water hit my skin, I relaxed and smiled. Seeing Beauty up with her .22 made me happy because she was just like me.

"Bout time you got back." I loved the sound of Ced's voice, so deep, smooth and sexy.

"How long you been up?"

"The shower water woke me up," he said with a perfect white smile. He looked at my body boldly, and I knew he knew I was his.

"Wanna join me?" I hoped he said yes.

He let his boxers hit the floor and I had to bite down on my bottom lip because his body was *priceless.* He was cut in all the right places, just like a diamond.

As he entered the shower, all I could do was shake my head. I only had one thought running through my mind right then, *Cold-hearted or not, I am one lucky bitch.*

Chapter 20
Dead Men Can't Talk

"Baby, answer your phone." Ced nudged me awake.

This better be something good, because I am fucking tired, I thought. My body was sore from last night's love making. I answered without looking to see who was calling,

"Yo."

"Babyma, wake up."

"Nigga, what fuckin' time is it?" I asked, mad as hell.

"Mane, it's 6:45 in the morning."

"Well, what the fuck you want?" I was super pissed the fuck off. *6:45? This better not be no bullshit.*

"I just blast me a nigga."

His words put steel in my back and I was suddenly sitting straight the fuck up in bed, with Ced looking at me all puzzled the fuck out. "Nigga, you what?" I asked him to make sure I was hearing him right.

"Mane, I gotta leave town, yo."

"Nigga, chill out, you trippin' for nothin'." I could tell his heart wasn't cold. "Where you at?"

I could hear him breathing real hard in the phone, but he wasn't talking. I needed that nigga to get it together.

"Yo," I barked into the phone.

"I fucked up, yo."

Now he sounded scared, and I knew that meant trouble.

"Who was you with?" I was hoping he said by himself. *Please say you were alone*, I thought.

"My nigga Top."

Yup, he had fucked up. Niggas couldn't hold no water, they were worse than a bitch.

"He still with you?" I was praying to God he told me yes.

"Yea."

"Where y'all at?"

As he told me, I jumped out of my bed and put my clothes from the previous night back on.

"A'ite, stay there." I ended the call.

Ced was up and looking at me as I pulled my Timbs on, but I didn't even let him ask me anything. I just started talking, "Dumb ass done blasted a nigga with one of his homeboys. He's at the Hampton Inn."

"So you captain save a hoe now?"

I couldn't believe that nigga had said that, but he did.

"Call it what you want. I'll be back." I didn't give him a chance to respond.

All kinds of things were running through my head, along with Ced's comment.

Yea, I knew I had no business fucking with Traymon on that level, but I felt like I had to because he was the father of my child. Beauty deserved to have her dad. If I had to help make that happen, I was going to ride for mine.

I got out around Ward's Rd., but I didn't go to the Hampton. I called T.

"Yo, I'm here, but I want you to come to the Pizza Hut," I told him as soon as he answered his phone. No way in hell was I pulling up in that bitch when I knew they had cameras.

Pizza Hut was just across the street.

"Damn," I said out loud, wondering what the fuck was going on with T.

Ace Hood's song *Ride* went off on my phone, alerting me that I had a text message from Ced.

As I read it, a smile broke out on my face. "Be Careful."

I texted him back saying, "Thanks, Daddy."

I hit send when I saw T and Top walking towards my car. I must say that T was looking good. Those fifteen days in rehab had cleaned him up pretty well. Top was tall, at least six feet and over two hundred pounds, and his weight looked good on him. He was wearing a black t-shirt, with a dark blue pair of jeans, along with some black dopemans. For a dark-skinned nigga, he looked okay.

"What's good with you?" Top asked me from the back seat after he got in.

Traymon got in the front with me.

"Nothin'. Just livin'," I replied.

Traymon was holding his head with both hands. He must've been stressed the fuck out.

I put the car in drive and pulled off onto the main street.

"So what's the deal?" I asked breaking the silence between us.

Traymon leaned his head on the head rest and looked over at me, but I was looking at Top in my mirror. He was just looking out the window as I drove. I wondered if he was just playing it cool.

"So, last night my nigga calls me and was like, 'I heard you snitched on this nigga Q back in the day.' I'm like, 'What the fuck you talkin' 'bout?'"

I took my eyes off the road for a second to glance at Traymon, and his eyebrows were pushed together.

"He's like yea, the nigga Ray say you told on his cousin Q back in the day."

I didn't know none of those niggas, so it must have been before my time with T.

"Babyma, you know for yourself I ain't never snitched on no nigga, so for the nigga to drop a lie like that on me pissed me off. The nigga's tryin' to ruin my reputation and label me as a snitch. Once you have that label on you, it's *over*, because somebody knows something or they're just hating hard, but either way you're fucked. Anyway, I run into this nigga Ray on the block. I'm like 'Yo, you claim I told on your peoples back in the day, where you get that from?' The nigga gonna tell me somebody told him. He's on that he said she said bullshit. But for real, the nigga's mad 'cause I fucked his bitch 'bout two months ago, you feel me?"

That nigga still couldn't keep his dick in his pants for nothin'. No wonder he had drama.

"To make a long story short, you hurt his ego." I hit the nail on the head and I knew it.

"But to say I'm snitchin', what the fuck?" he said with a chuckle.

"It is what it is. The nigga's dead now, so he can't spread no more rumors," Top put in from the back seat.

I shook my head, but I didn't say anything. I knew it was time to go to the mountain.

***

I parked the car in the same place I always did. I got out first, Traymon next, and Top followed. I lifted my face to the sky. The view up there was beautiful, but they both seemed to be in a daze.

Traymon was to my left and Top was to my right. I pulled my baby from my back and fired two shots into his head, *pointblank*.

His body hit the ground hard. His head was open and its contents were pouring everywhere. It was a puddle of Top juice. He never expected that, and that's just the way I liked it. The sound of his body hitting the ground made Traymon jump.

"What the fuck?" his scream filled my ears.

"Nigga, don't question my actions." He was a dumb ass nigga for real. How the fuck was he gonna smoke one nigga in front of another nigga and think he was gonna be walking free?

"You must want a codefendant," I told him as I opened the door of the car.

He jerked back at my words like I'd slapped him. "He ain't like that."

I turned around to look at him just to make sure I was hearing him clearly.

"So you tellin' me you know what the next man is capable of doin'? If he was like that he ain't now. Now he's gonna be good and quiet. Dead niggas don't tell secrets."

He was looking at the body, just shaking his head like it was all a dream. I got in the car and closed the door. *He better hurry up and get the fuck in before I leave him looking more stupid than he already does,* I thought.

He got in the car and I pulled away, leaving Top to the crows for breakfast, lunch, and dinner, buffet style. I hoped those motherfuckers were hungry because that was a lot of meat.

"You let another nigga see you in action. What the fuck was you thinkin'?" I asked after he got into the passenger seat. He didn't answer, didn't even look at me, so I continued.

"Then you puttin' your freedom in his hands, talkin' bout he ain't like that. Niggas rotate every second and they'll tell on their own damn momma. What makes you think you safe and you ain't even blood?"

That nigga needed to be schooled because his ignorance was gonna kill him. He shook his head, once again, but said nothing.

"And what about Beauty, nigga? What about your daughter? Witnesses put people in jail. You gonna get locked up and take her Daddy away?" I was getting mad and yelling at him. He was fucking with my daughter's life.

He better start talking before I send his ass with Top. Fuck some Golden Corral. It's gonna be Dummy Corral up on this mountain if he don't get it together. These crows gonna be eating good today.

"You done this before?" he asked me.

Shit, if he was gonna start asking questions, he could keep his mouth shut. I thought he would've had more to say than a question mark.

"Don't ask me no questions," I snapped at him. I hated when motherfuckers asked me questions like that, or questioned my actions. I ran me, and I didn't answer to nobody.

"Where you wanna be dropped off at?" I asked. I was ready to get away from his ass.

"Take me to my crib." He just shook his head. Damn, the nigga was doing so much shaking I was starting to wonder if he had Parkinson's.

I hit the highway bumping Jeezy's *Can't Ban the Snowman*.

I pulled up in, front of Traymon's house fifteen minutes and a few songs later.

"You know that was Talena's brother?"

I looked at him and smiled. Knowing that I had just touched her family made me happy. Of all the things he could've said, I didn't see that one coming.

"No witnesses around, better chance of livin'," I told him as he exited the car. Fuck that bitch and her family, for real.

Chapter 21
Blood Hound

Ced was up and so were the kids. I could smell food and my stomach growled, even though I was not hungry.

"Good morning everyone," I said to the kids as I entered the kitchen.

"Morning," they said in unison. Everybody was at the table eating, except Ced, who'd already started on the dishes.

"Hey, baby," I said to Ced. He was up to his elbows in soap bubbles.

"Hey, boo," he smiled and I knew he was happy to see me home in one piece. His smile said it all, and I couldn't help but give him one of my own.

I left them and headed towards the stairs, but I heard footsteps behind me, so I turned around to see who it was. Beauty. When I got to my room, Beauty came in and closed the door behind her.

"Ma, you sure stay busy with handling your business. When do you even sleep?"

"Mommy gets enough sleep, boo," I told her as a way to slide by the rest of her statement.

"I'm just glad that you're back," she said as she kissed my face.

"I am *always* comin' back home to you. Don't ever question that."

"Whenever you leave to go handle your business, just tell me, please." She showed me her perfect pretty smile and I smiled just the same. She was the beat of my heart.

"I will."

Just like that, she left the room to give me some space. I took my clothes off and headed to the shower for the second time in less than eight hours.

Ced was in the room when I got out of the shower. "I know you still love him."

"You can't be serious."

We were face to face and his eyes were red. It looked like he'd been crying.

"Why would you say something like that?"

"Cause you always down for that nigga."

"I am down for the nigga 'cause he is Beauty's father. You do shit for your kids' mom 'cause that's their mother. It doesn't mean you love her. Or do you?"

"I have love for her 'cause she birthed my kids."

"Well, that's how I feel."

Ced was territorial, and I loved that he loved me that way, but I didn't want him to be jealous for real, because there was no reason for it.

"You're my man, my soon to be husband, and no one can or will take your place," I said to him as I held his face in my hands. "I'm there for him 'cause of Beauty. I'm not jealous because you're there for your kids' ma. I respect you for that, so respect me also. My heart is yours, and my body belongs to you, so don't ever say I love him again."

He kissed my lips and I allowed his tongue to roam my mouth. He tasted good, but I had to pull away because the kids were awake.

"Give me some real quick," he said with a sad puppy face.

"No." He hated it when I told him no. I left him standing there with his sad puppy face.

"You just a blood hound for this pussy," I said with a laugh.

He walked towards the door and stopped.

"Yea, just a blood hound for you." He closed the door behind him and I couldn't help but smile because he was telling the truth.

Chapter 22
Blessed

I loved spending time with the kids. They were so full of energy, full of life and promise. Just seeing them happy made me happy.

I'd come to a point where I was glad that I'd been through all the shit I'd been through because I knew I'd die protecting them from any danger or unhappiness.

Ced's love was real and pure. He'd shown me that not all men were dogs. His love for me had fixed my heart in so many ways, and for that I was blessed. He was known by many, understood by few, and loved only by the *real*. I was grateful it was a new day and I was blessed.

Jamaica

Chapter 23
On that Level

Ced's children were back with their mother, Beauty was at school, and Ced was handling business with his crew, so I was home alone, enjoying the house by myself for a change, until my phone rang.

"Hello." I put my sexy voice on for my man.

"Yo, I heard somebody's throwin' slugs at your baby daddy."

"Where at, do you know?" I was up and getting myself ready before the question was completely out of my mouth.

"Over his way."

I was hoping Traymon was strapped and alive. Damn.

"A'ite. What you doin'?" I asked Ced to show him I was also concerned about him. Not everything was about T.

"Cooking fried Chicken." So he was in the trap, around the stove.

"Thanks, baby."

"Be careful, Sweets." I could hear the concern in his voice and it never failed to touch me.

"You know I will."

I hung up and dialed Traymon's number, but he didn't answer. *Mane, I hope this nigga is still living. There's gonna be hell to pay if he ain't*, I thought.

I was doing the speed limit because I knew I was super dirty. Boosie Bad Ass was jumping and I was in a zone. I couldn't even think right. As soon as I saw the Lynchburg exit, I relaxed because I was almost to my destination. Traymon was on my mind, and I hoped Beauty's nightmare hadn't come alive for real.

I got to the Bridge in minutes only to see that there were police every damn where. I parked the car in Johnson Health Center, but I left my best friend behind and walked to where the police were. The need for damage control said I had to be where the action was.

The entire neighborhood was outside trying to see what was going on. I spotted Regina in the crowd. I walked towards her. My cell phone vibrated, so I pulled it out of the pocket of my jeans and answered it.

"Yo."

"Yo, I'm lookin' at you right now."

I stopped dead in my tracks and looked around to see if I saw Traymon anywhere, but he was nowhere in sight. Regina spotted me and I saw her start walking towards me.

"Don't say shit to that bitch," T sounded pissed.

"Hey, girl," she said like we were friends.

I knew that bitch knew better, but I'd play her game. She knew the cost of fucking with me and mine.

"What's up?" I still had my phone on my ear while I was talking to her.

"I heard that the police lookin' for Traymon." I swear I saw a hint of a smile on her face.

"For what?"

"They say him and another person was shootin' at each other."

"Who the other person?" How the fuck was she gonna bring me half the damn story?

Traymon was still on the phone and I was pretty sure he could hear our conversation.

"I don't know," she said like she didn't give a fuck.

"When you hear from T, let him know I'm worried about him." Her face dropped. I still had that effect on her ass with my words. Dumb bitch.

"I sure will," she said with an attitude and walked off.

As I walked back to my car, I tried not to laugh, but I couldn't help it. She knew who was running shit, and I was never gonna let her forget it.

"Yo, that nigga Jay came through here blastin'." I heard Traymon loud and clear. Jay finally had some balls. I wondered who he stole them from.

"And?"

"Babyma, you know I stay strapped and on point. I sent his ass some heat back."

"I'm glad you did."

"Ain't no pussy in my blood. I have a feelin' that bitch set me up, too. Mane, I'm in JP's house lookin' at these clowns," He said with a laugh, and I laughed with him.

"Now you on that level I've always wanted you on nigga," I told him as I opened the car door.

"Thanks for always runnin' to help rescue a nigga, yo."

"Real recognize real, I'll never rotate on you."

"I already know." I could hear the confidence in his response when he said that.

"Hit me up later. I gotta pick Beauty up from school."

"Love you, Babyma."

"Nigga, you only love my gangsta side," I sang into the phone.

He laughed at me, and that caused me to laugh also.

"Hit me up later. I'mma lay low for a minute."

I ended the call and pulled out of the Center. *Damn. I gotta drop this joint off.* I called Ced and let him know I was on my way to him.

***

"I'm outside."

"A'ite."

Even in the trap that nigga stayed looking good. My pussy was wet just like that. *Damn,*

I might be dick whipped.

"You good?" he asked me after he got in the passenger seat.

I gave him the rundown, but when I said Jay's name, his whole face dropped, and he didn't even comment.

"I gotta pick Beauty up from school, and I can't drive around with this." I pull my .9 and hold it in my lap.

He smiled at me, reaching into my lap to get my baby.

"Make sure you keep her safe." I put my hand on his and he gave me that perfect smile that I love so much. It was a gift every day, and it was better than diamonds.

"Anything for my Queen."

"Give me some sugar." I leaned into him and without question he did as he was told. Our lips made music together and I loved it.

"Don't make me put these niggas out, 'cause you know I'm a blood hound for that pussy."

He killed me with that smile, and I wished I could've given him some. I knew he would've gotten it, but then I would've been running late to get Beauty, and nothing came before her, not even him.

"I'll let you get a sample later. I've got to go get Beauty," I said with a serious face.

"Let me know when you get home."

"You know I will."

***

I parked outside the school, waiting for Beauty to come running through the door like she always did. I turned the radio to 97.5 to hear the news replay from earlier that day.

"News at 3 is brought to you by McDonalds. I'm LaQuiva Cashwell reporting to you from 97.5 FM. Fifty-two year old Silvia Jones was found dead in her living room by her son Mr. Jahmain "Jay" Jones. No witnesses have come forward, and right now the residents on Sussex Street are asking for help. When asked about Silvia Jones, her neighbor called her a good hearted woman, and said she couldn't believe she was gone. Not even an hour ago police were called to Timbridge Hill, also known as The Bridge, about a shootout. No one was injured in that situation but officers are still investigating."

Damn, Jay found his mom. I knew he was hurting, and I was loving it. He deserved every ounce of pain I could give him before I took his life. Nigga should've gotten shit right the first time and made sure I was dead, because I was going after everyone and everything he loved.

If the police were still investigating the shootout, why the fuck did Regina say that they were looking for Traymon? I was really starting to hate that bitch with a passion.

I changed the station as soon as I saw Beauty coming towards the car. I stepped out to greet my princess with my arms open, knowing she'd fly into them.

"Mom, you look beautiful," she said.

"Thank you, boo, and so do you." I squeezed her tight before letting her go.

"You ain't know? I got it from my momma." We both laugh when she said her two cents worth.

I cherished moments like that, and I wouldn't have traded them for anything. I was glad that I was teaching her to be on that level like me.

Jamaica

Chapter 24
Why?

I text Ced as soon as we walked through the front door. He responded by calling me.

"You want me to bring that too?" I knew he was referring to my .9.

"You damn right. I'm already feelin' naked."

"A'ite, I'll be there soon, Sweets. I love you."

"I love you also, Mr. Williams."

I ended the call quickly, because I needed to start fixing dinner for my family. Beauty was already in her room, but I yelled for her to come back downstairs so we could talk. Shrimp Alfredo was gonna have to do. It didn't matter what I cooked, they'd eat it.

"Yes, Ma?"

"How is school goin'?"

"School is going good. We supposed to be getting our report cards next week," she stated as she plopped herself in a chair at the kitchen table.

"Are you failin' any classes?"

"Ma," she said to me with some bass in her voice.

I stopped cutting up onions to look at her.

"Ma, I ain't failin' nothin', straight A's baby right here," she pointed at herself like I didn't know who she was talking about.

It didn't matter what was going on, when she was around, she kept a smile on my face.

"I'm just makin' sure, boo," I said, winking at her

"Let me borrow your phone so I can call my daddy."

"The phone's right there on the table, his name is under…"

"Babydaddy," she finished my sentence.

I know this child of mines didn't just cut me off, I thought to myself. I continued to fix our dinner as she strolled into the living room with my phone.

"Daddy, what you doin'?"

I blocked her conversation out by turning on the radio. She was starting to get older, and I knew she needed some space. I wasn't trying to be all up in her conversation like that. Tamia's I'm Still was playing. My body was there, in the kitchen, but my mind was far away.

Why did Jay shoot after Traymon? I wondered if he knew that I'd killed his mother. I did know one thing though, he better had stayed far away from my child and my man, because there'd be hell to pay if he didn't.

"Ma, Daddy wants to talk to you," Beauty handed me the phone and walked out of the kitchen.

"Yea, I forgot to tell you that bitch Dimples was drivin' that nigga today."

"Dimples?" I asked just to make fucking sure I was hearing that right.

"Mane, I seen that bitch with my own damn eyes. She was laughin' the whole damn time, but when I got cover and started bustin' back, the bitch sped off with Jay hangin' out the window."

I had to find those two real fast before I lost someone real close to me. I knew Dimples had probably put Talena up on game. She'd probably told Jay, and since he was fucking with Regina, he was more than likely getting information out of that bitch about me and Traymon. The shit was getting complicated.

"Babyma, you even listenin' to me?"

"Huh?" I was so lost in my thoughts that I didn't even know what else he'd said. My head was busy calculating these complications. People were about to be subtracted from the equation.

"Just be careful. I'm layin' low for a minute. Kiss my daughter for me."

"A'ite." I ended the call and stirred the shrimp, only to see that one side had burned while I was on the phone. Damn. Why the fuck did I keep letting those motherfuckers live when they didn't deserve to breathe? I needed to show them all that I was *not* the one to be played with.

"Damn, baby, you alright?" All white everything and quiet as a ghost, I didn't hear Ced come into the house. His voice startled me, jerking me out of my thoughts. He saw me jump.

"I'm gonna be alright, don't even question that. I'm ready to turn the fuck up though." I was serious as a heart attack, and he knew it, but I knew he wouldn't question me. I had to move before those motherfuckers got to talking and plotting. Hell naw.

"Look, I need your help." I'd never said those words to him before, even though he'd offered help. I could handle me alone, but this time it was different. This was turning into a *family* thing.

Ced smiled, and it did two things at once. Even though it had been a few years, it still made my heart skip a beat, but it also said he was down and ready.

"Name it. You know I got you."

"I've gotta get Beauty to Bella's house first, then I'mma need you to ride."

"Say no more, baby. I got your back."

After I finished cooking dinner, I sat down with Beauty and Ced at the table and we ate together. I told Beauty she had to stay with Bella for a week and she was down with the idea because the other kids, her cousins, would be there. I also told her not to worry about me because I was going to be okay.

Ced promised her that on Friday he would get his kids, and we'd all go out of town for the weekend. Her face was covered with a huge smile as soon as he said that.

Family came first, even when it meant getting your hands dirty, and my hands loved it, especially when my life was on the line.

Jamaica

Chapter 25
Killa Sweets on Monday

We dropped Beauty off around 9pm with a bag full of clothes since she'd be going to school from her grandmother's house. I told Bella that I was going out of town, and that I expect to be back on Friday to get her. I gave her two stacks also. It didn't hurt to go above and beyond for those who did for me and mine. I'd always take care of Bella.

"You don't have to pay me to watch her, Sweets, she is my grandchild."

"Don't think I am tryin' to disrespect you, Bella, but the least I can do is help out."

She smiled at me and walked off, giving me and Beauty some time together before I left.

"Remember everythin' I've told you." I traced the middle part in her braids with one finger as she looked up at me.

"Ma, I've got it locked in my head. Just make sure you get back to me, or this place is gonna see Lil Sweets in action." Her voice was low but solid, and the emotion behind her words was intense. Her response made me smile. I was glad that she was my child. I wouldn't have traded her for anything.

She left me at the car, and I watched as she entered the house, closing the door behind her.

When I got inside the car, Ced was looking at me with disbelief. I knew he'd heard our conversation, and truth be told, I didn't care.

If he ever left it up to me, his kids would have a heart just like mines.

"She's gonna be just like you, Sweets."

I put the car in drive and pulled away from the curb.

"I hope she turns out better."

I turned the music up. I was not even in the mood to hear what else he had to say. My daughter *would* be better. I intended to see to it. She'd be *smarter, stronger, and colder*.

Jeezy said it best, "I got the weight of the world on my shoulders, and I swear it feels like ten thousand boulders, and it's so heavy, but I am so ready. Feels like I was born for this, if not, at least I'll die for it. They say I couldn't do it, but I still try for it. The big question is what can I do for you? Everybody lying to them, so I told them the truth."

I drove to Ced's apartment to get myself ready and get my mind right.

"What you need me to do?" Ced asked me as I cleaned my best friend up.

"Find me a low key car. Make sure everythin' on the joint is legal, too." I put the clip into the .9, and smiled when I heard it click as I put one in the chamber. Ced shook his head and smiled. Who is this woman? His smile seemed to say. It wasn't the first time he'd seen me in action.

I was so ready to get my hands dirty again that the fingers on my right hand wouldn't stop twitching. I wondered briefly if I was addicted to pulling the trigger. I didn't think there was a rehab for that. I wouldn't have wanted it anyway, and it was not like I was out of control.

Ced had called one of his boys and had him drop a car off outside. I could say one thing, Ced and his crew moved fast.

"You ready, daddy?" I asked him, even though I know he was crunk and happy that I was taking him on this journey with me.

We were both in all black, sharper than a dead motherfucker in a casket. I looked Ced up and down. He looked just as good in all black as he did in all white, and he was so sexy it took my breath away.

I knew I was one lucky bitch, for real.

"Ready as you are," he answered without hesitation.

I checked the time on my black G-Shock and it said 12:45am. It was time to move. I'd always come through for Traymon, so he damn well better had come through for me.

It was wet outside, but the storm only seemed to make the night more beautiful to me. I heard thunder growling deep and dangerous a split second before lightening ripped the night sky in two. Between the darkness and the pouring rain, we had excellent cover for a drive.

The lights in the house were off. I didn't pull into their driveway. I parked on the street instead.

"I'll be back."

"I thought we was doin' this together?"

"We are, Ced. Just stay here, and I'll be back."

I made sure my baby was tucked in my back before easing out of the car and closing the door softly. The lights from the car were off, even though the engine was still running. It seemed the closer I got to the house, the more my fingers twitched. I took a deep breath and exhaled slowly in an effort to calm them. I was soaking wet just from that short distance between the door and the curb.

I twisted 'the knob on the door and it turned. *Nice job, T*, I thought to myself. I pushed the door closed, but I didn't throw the deadbolt. I pulled my phone out and touched the screen so I could use it to give me some light.

"The bedroom is the second door on the left," I heard Traymon's voice in my head.

I held my breath for a second before I pushed the door open. The hinges squeaked as it swung open, and the body in the bed shifted slightly, disturbed by the sound. I pulled my gun from behind me and walked towards the bed, after I put my phone in my pocket. I let my eyes adjust to the darkness, and I didn't move until I could see clearly. But when I could, I put the cold steel in her back. She turned on her side, startled and confused, trying to make sense of what was happening. The bitch didn't have no survival skills.

"Let's go, bitch," I delivered my words forcefully. She needed to know this wasn't a joke.

I knew she knew my voice, and she knew she better not play with me, especially when I had a gun in my hand.

"Where's your phone at?"

"Please don't kill me." She was begging already.

"Don't make me ask you again."

"By the T.V stand."

I glanced at the T.V. stand real quick to see for myself.

"Get the fuck up and let's go."

"I need to get dressed," she whined. She was wearing a white t-shirt that came down to her knees. Good enough.

"Bitch. Let's. Go." She was making me fucking mad.

I grabbed her phone off the stand as we exited the bedroom, and put it in my pocket along with mine. I had the joint pushed against her back, and her fear had her walking straight as an arrow. She better not have tried anything crazy. But if she did, it wouldn't change the end result. I had my mind made up, and I would be leaving there satisfied, end of story.

I pushed her out of the front door into what was left of the storm.

She used her hands to cover her head from the drizzle, but continued to walk towards the car like a good dog. Ced was in the driver seat, just as I'd planned.

"Open the back door and get in," I ordered that scary ass bitch. With trembling hands, she complied.

Deep down I think she already knew that she didn't have any choices left. From that point on, I'd be making her choices for her. Ced didn't even give me enough time to close the door. He pulled off as soon as I climbed in beside her. I still had the joint pointed at her, only now it was aimed at her heart.

I wondered if Ced was nervous about this whole situation, but as I had explained it all to him earlier, he had to *trust* my actions.

"Shut. The. Fuck. Up," I screamed, pushing the joint all up in her face. I was getting tired of hearing that bitch cry.

"Please don't kill me, I am pregnant," she wailed.

That made me laugh out loud. I hoped she knew who the father was so I could pay my respects in person. There would be one less disloyal baby around, like mother, like child.

I'd never seen Regina so scared before, and I must admit that I liked her that way. This was even better than the day I beat her ass in the middle of her own kitchen.

She moved her legs restlessly, shaking them back and forth so that her knees banged together each time they closed. She shook them fast, then slow, then fast again, and even that was getting on my fucking nerves.

I'd known this day would eventually come, and I felt *powerful* knowing that her life depended on me. I took the phones out of my pocket and threw mine into the front seat.

"You gonna call Traymon for me," I told her.

Her legs stopped shaking instantly. "Why?"

Her eyes were wide, face taut with terror.

I truly *hated* when motherfuckers questioned my commands. I was the *fucking boss*.

She read my face correctly for a change and once again begged for her life.

"Please. I'll do anything. Just don't kill me."

Her tears traced twin rivers down her cheeks and I couldn't hold my smile.

Beg, Bitch.

The car stopped, and I knew we'd reached Holland Mills Park, which was really just an over-grown picnic area where people could also fish if they wanted to.

"Please, please," she cried, holding her hands out to me in supplication.

Ced turned around to face her. "Get your soul right 'cause your end is near," he told her with a smile on his face.

I wondered for a moment if my smile was as *cold* as his when he looked at her.

Her face dropped like she knew he was telling the truth and there was no escape. She closed her eyes, so I gave her a minute to say what she had to say to God, in case that was what she was doing. *She better make it good and quick,* I thought.

I pushed the phone into her hand so she could call Traymon like I told her.

"What have I done to deserve, this?"

"Loyalty is a *must*, it's a *lifestyle*." I saw understanding dawn on her face. Now it was all making sense to her. She rotated on my baby's daddy when he needed her the most. That decision was gonna cost her more than she wanted to pay, and I was there to collect.

She scrolled through her contacts to Traymon's name.

She put the phone to her ear and waited on him to pick up. The volume was clearly on high because I could hear it ringing. After five rings, he finally answered.

She took a deep breath before she spoke.

"Please don't do this to me." She lost her composure and suddenly she was crying again.

"Some battles you can win, but this one you can't." He disconnected, and the phone went dead in her hand.

Ced was out of the car, waiting to open the door on her side.

"Let me get the phone," I told her calmly.

She gave it up quickly. Her door opened and I nodded at her, telling her to move.

Ced had his .45 pointed at her head as I exited the car behind her.

144

"We gonna take a walk to the river." I knew my voice sounded *cold*, but it was only honest.

"Please. I am beggin' you," she screamed with tears running down her cheeks.

That bitch knew me. It didn't matter how loud she got, *no one* would be able to hear her with all the lightening and thundering going on. Ced placed the .45 behind her head as I stepped in front of her to take the lead.

Twenty steps later, I could see the water reflecting the lightening in the sky. It was beautiful out there at that time of night with or without the rain. The river was swollen from the storm and it almost looked like it was about to overflow.

"Regina." I stopped and turned to her so she could see my face. "This shit between us is personal, way too deep, and I don't appreciate you tryin' to set up Traymon, knowin' that Beauty cherishes the ground he walks on."

She tried to speak, but I put my burner to her head and she stopped.

"Tell Top hello for me."

Ced had walked off, leaving us to talk.

She was shocked to hear me say that, but I bet she wasn't surprised when I pulled the trigger twice. She knew that I was a woman of my word, and my actions proved it. The silencer attached to my .9 drowned out the sound. I watched as her body crumpled into the water. It only took a few seconds for the current to carry her away.

Jamaica

Chapter 26
Tuesday

The cable box said the time was 11:49am, eleven minutes away from the midday news, but I was not even going to watch it. Fuck giving that bitch some respect.

Ced was still asleep. Just looking at him gave me a reason to smile. I listened to the sound of him breathing, and I couldn't help but think that God couldn't have created him for anyone else but me because together we were prefect. Nothing else made sense. I eased my way out of bed, grabbed my cell phone from the T.V. stand and walked to the bathroom to release my bladder.

As soon as I sat on the cold ass toilet seat, I pressed two on my phone. It rang into my ear and I relaxed my muscles to let the water flow, from my pussy lips.

"What's crackin' nigga?" I asked when I heard his voice.

"Shit, just chillin', waitin' for the midday news to come on."

"Well, I am just checkin' up on you." I wasn't trying to interrupt his time with his ol' lady. The news report was all they had left.

"Where our daughter at?"

"School, you know education is the key to life." Just like that, we shared a laugh together.

Surviving is the motherfucking key to life, fuck education, truth be told.

"Keep her safe, Sweets."

"I'll die makin' sure she is safe at all times. Don't ever think I'll let someone hurt her."

"You're a great mother." He breathed hard into the phone before he continued, "I just want to tell you thank you for everything you've done for me.

This time I knew the nigga wasn't turning soft, but his voice sounded weak and worn out. I knew he was hurting. And although he didn't want to acknowledge it, I knew he was missing me and what he could've had, but I was not trying to hear that shit so I told him, "Hit me up later and duck them haters."

"Already, Babyma."

I ended the call before he tried to say anything else. I didn't have time for hearing that shit anyway. He had to get his emotions under control fast. I'd done all I could for him.

I washed my hands, brushed my teeth, and headed towards the kitchen to fix something to eat. After last night's work out of spilling blood, on top of Ced fucking me to sleep, my stomach was growling like a werewolf. French toast with scrambled eggs would fix that noise that it was making, but first I had to call Bella and check up on Beauty.

"Hey Lady," she answered the call and it made me smile.

"How you doing?"

"Good. Sittin' here getting' ready to watch the midday news."

Damn, a lot of people must watch the midday news.

"Oh, okay," I said, brushing the subject off.

"You gonna pick Beauty up from school?" I asked, even though I knew she would. But I still wanted to know for sure. Sometimes you just had to hear something with your own ears.

"You know I am." I could hear her laughing.

"A'ite then, Bella. Thanks a lot."

"No problem, Sweets." I could hear the T.V. in the background. "Today's midday news is brought to you by…"

I ended the call to start making my breakfast. Even over all the noise that I was making in the kitchen, I could hear Ced moving around in the bedroom. After a few minutes, I heard him talking on his phone.

"My nigga, that shit was supposed to be handled a long time ago." He sounded irritated with whoever was on the phone with him. "How the fuck you just now bringin' that shit back to my attention?"

As I scrambled the eggs, I made sure not to make any out the way noise because I was trying to hear what he was saying.

"Don't even worry about it. Just send me the info and I'll handle the shit my damn self."

I needed to know what was going the fuck on.

"Naw, I'mma do it."

I could hear him even better. He sounded like he was heading towards me.

"A'ite." He was in the kitchen with me now. I turned around to see my man and I was proud to say how sexy my man looked just getting out of bed.

He was wearing an all-white wife beater, with blue polo shorts and his white polo slippers. His dreads were pulled out of his face towards the back.

"Mornin', daddy."

He took a step towards me and smiled to make my heart melt. He kissed my lips and I couldn't help but let his tongue dance in my mouth. When he pulled away, I gave him a sad face like *why'd you stop?*

He laughed at me and said, "Don't burn the eggs."

I turn around quickly. Damn. I'd lost my appetite for food just like that. Now I was feening for more of his lips. I removed the eggs from the pan and split them between two separate plates. Ced was sitting at the table watching me move around the kitchen. I knew that my pink boy shorts had gotten his attention because they cuffed my ass nicely, along with my baby t-shirt. I played a little, clapping my ass for him.

"Don't think I can't eat you and breakfast at the same time."

I smiled and put his plate in front of him. I knew he'd put the French toast and eggs all over my body and eat it off of me one bite at a time.

"Don't let me try you." I winked at him in a sexy way. He returned my smile, but I knew my man, and I could tell something heavy was on his mind.

I fixed my plate and took a seat in front of him, hoping he'd talk to me. He kept his eyes on the table for a second then lifted his head up and breathed heavy. Fuck waiting on him to tell me what was going on. I asked him.

"What's wrong, baby?"

The food smelled good, but my man's problems came first. He looked at me and once again gave me that perfect smile.

"A month ago, a nigga from Alabama opened up shop here. I told Trigger to handle the situation, but he says he can't really get close enough to deal with this nigga."

All I can do is shake my head. I took my first bite of food, and watched Ced watching me.

"Keep talkin', but eat too, so your food doesn't get cold before you get to it."

He lifted his fork and sliced into a piece of the French toast.

"Them niggas scared, talkin' bout how hot the city is with all these dead bodies." He brought his fork to his mouth.

"Fuck they worried about that for?" I asked. "As long as it ain't them, why are they worried about the city bleeding?"

He shook his head like he didn't know, so I continued, "You have all the info on the nigga?"

He nodded his head, his mouth too full to speak.

"I'll handle it for you, daddy. Just give me what I need."

He knew all I need was an address and a description, or even a name, and the situation would be handled.

He pushed his phone over to me. I needed to get myself one of those soon. The HTC flat screen phone was sexy. It had *boss* written all over it. The screen had all the information that I needed, address, name, height, weight. I mean the whole damn report was right there.

"Why you didn't run this by me before Ced?"

He looked at me. "You have your own thing goin' on, Sweets."

That motherfucker didn't understand that his problems *were* mines.

"We're one. What you go through, I go through too." I was upset that he said I had my own problems to handle after all the other shit I'd handled for him.

He knew I was pissed, so he didn't speak.

I cleared my plate and left it at the table. I had to walk away before I said something I'd regret.

I took my clothes off once I reached the bathroom. I needed a shower, I had to clear my head.

This new nigga stayed on Blue Ridge Street, he was five feet eleven inches, two hundred twenty-five pounds with dreads, and he went by the name *Quick*. No wonder them niggas couldn't get him, his name must've been a description of his actions. Well, he hadn't met me yet, but he would very soon.

My eyes were closed as the water ran through my hair onto my skin. I didn't know Ced had entered the bathroom, much less the shower, until his hands touched my breasts.

I opened my eyes and stared into his before I lowered my gaze to his body. Damn. He was so sexy, with dreads hanging just right above his six pack, and the tool swinging between his legs took my breath away. My mind was still upset, but my pussy was saying something different.

"Don't be upset with me." His eyes were begging me for forgiveness, and the way he was making my body feel by playing with my nipples, I'd already forgiven him.

He gently pulled on my nipples and I stepped closer to him. He put his lips on mine and I was ready to surrender. I relaxed and let my pussy take control of my mind. He pulled away from me, lowering his mouth to my breasts. His lips took my left nipple and I dropped my head back in pleasure. The warm sensation between my legs had me weak already. He treated my right nipple the same way he treated my left.

Moans escaped from my lips. I couldn't help it, my body was on fire for him and the shower couldn't put it out. He used his tongue to travel down to my navel, and then dropped to his knees. I tried to back up, but he spoke, "Don't move."

My eyes were closed but my ears were open. I could feel his breath close to my pussy. When his tongue met my clit, it felt so good. He started to move it back and forth and I spread my legs wider to give him space. He licked from my pussy to my ass and I couldn't help the way I was feeling, so I came all in his mouth. He looked up and smiled at me.

He turned me around, with the warm water running over both of us. He lifted my left leg as he positioned himself behind me. I arched my back so I could welcome his dick as he entered me. I pushed back with force once he was inside me. I wanted to fuck. I looked back and could tell by his facial expression that he loved what I was doing. I braced myself against the wall as he drove into me.

"Don't stop," I cried out to him. I was already on the edge of another nut. He was giving me full strokes, nice long, hard ones. He put his thumb in my ass and that was all it took to send me over the edge. He stroked me faster and harder. He slapped my ass with his other hand, and then I felt him stiffen and relax as he released his cum into me.

We were both so out of breath that we stayed that way for a second.

I spoke first.

"You really know how to make me forgive you, huh?"

"You know I'm big daddy," he said, slapping my ass one more time before he moved.

152

We washed each other from head to toe and then we started round two, only this time we'd be going to the bedroom for more space. We fucked for almost three hours before we finally drifted off to sleep.

The sound of my phone woke me up. I looked at the cable box and it was 5:30pm. I jumped out of bed and dashed to the kitchen to answer it. Ced was out cold. My pussy had put his ass to sleep for real.

"Hello?" I answered, out of breath.

"Ma, what you doing?"

"Bout to clean up the kitchen."

"Oh, okay," she said like she cared.

"How was school?"

"It was good. We're supposed to take a Math test tomorrow."

"Make sure you study so you can get a good grade."

"I will."

I am standing in the kitchen naked as ever, but I figured I may as well start cleaning it or make myself a liar.

"Where's your grandma at?"

"In the kitchen, you wanna talk to her?"

"Yea. I love you, Beauty."

"I love you too, Ma. I am going outside with my cousins to play."

"Have fun." Damn, the kitchen was a mess. I started wiping down the counters.

"Hello?"

"Hey, Bella."

"You know that girl Traymon was messin' with is dead?" She wasted no time asking me.

"Huh?" I was playing dumb, but I had a smile on my face.

"Yea. They found her body in the James River early this morning." Damn, I didn't even think about the fact that Holland's

Mill River connected to James River. That strong ass current pulled that bitch into a whole different river.

"Damn." I grabbed the broom from the utility closet and started sweeping the kitchen floor.

"It is a cold world out there. People don't care no more. They gotta have a cold heart to kill a pregnant woman."

"Damn." That was all I could say.

"That's the same thing I'm sayin'."

"We all gotta go one day, I guess."

Silence.

My comment must have thrown her the fuck off.

"But not like that, Sweets."

"Bella, when it's your day, it's your day."

She huffed into the phone and I knew her mind was doing over time, so I changed the subject quickly while I dumped the dustpan into the trash.

"Give Beauty a kiss for me, and thanks again for watchin' her."

"I will, and no problem."

I ended the call after that.

It was almost six o'clock when I put my phone down.

In need of clothes, I walked back to the bedroom to find something to put on. Ced was still knocked out. I pulled one of his white tees over my head and went back to the kitchen to finish cleaning up.

Twenty minutes later, the kitchen was clean, and I was sitting in the living room cleaning my best friend.

"How long you been up?"

"Almost an hour." My face was still on my gun as I inserted bullets into the clip.

"How many gloves you have on?"

"Two," I said without looking up at him.

He walked off, leaving me to do me, but he yelled from the kitchen.

"You want some chicken fingers?"

Thank God for pre-cooked food.

"Yea, fix me some," I yelled back to him.

My baby was ready to rock and roll. I had two special stops to make later that night and my baby was gonna act right as always. I loved my P89.

Them damn chicken fingers and some ranch hit the spot just right.

After our "dinner," we played the X-Box 360, and as always, he beat me. I couldn't stand football, but I played with him anyway.

***

It was midnight and we were blacked the fuck out from head to fucking toe. I had to finish what I'd started, and Ced was helping me.

I knew I was wrong for what I was about to do, leaving those babies without their parents, but I had to or it might've cost me my life.

Talena Holloway used to be my boss at Layers, but a lot had changed. Now I had to finish her. After killing her kids' father, I found out that she knew Dimples, and knowing someone that I was at war with was a *problem.*

She didn't live on Shaffer anymore. Because she needed help raising her kids, she'd moved into her mother's house on Hood St., which was funny as hell because that bitch wasn't hood. I was so ready to dead that bitch.

Their house was the last one on the left side, and I could see Twan's Caprice parked in the driveway.

"Drop me off here," I told Ced as he drove past the house.

"How long?"

"Ten minutes," I said with a laugh.

"Sweets, how fuckin' long?" He was mad because he knew it shouldn't take me that long.

I reached over and kissed his lips. "Two minutes, circle the block twice and I'll be done."

I hopped out the car as soon as he stopped, P89 in hand as I ran towards my victim's home. Face to face was how it was going down. As I walked up towards the driveway, my heart started beating triple time.

Mane, I've gotta knock on the door. That's my only way in without waking up the whole house, I thought. "Fuck," I cursed myself quietly.

As I climbed the steps that led to the front door, I could feel my heart beating. The pressure of the situation just made it more exciting, but I was praying that the kids were asleep because I was not trying to hurt no kids.

Bam. Bam. Bam.

I knocked on the door and waited.

I counted down in my head before I knocked again. I'd give it ten seconds, ten, nine, eight, seven, six, five...

"Who the hell is it?"

Just the voice I wanted to hear.

"Dimples," I replied quickly.

The knob on the door was turning and my gun was aimed. As soon as the door opened, my finger pulled the trigger twice. Before her body even hit the floor, I was gone.

I met Ced at the top of the block. He spotted me running in the middle of the street and picked me up. Thank goodness I was in shape because that was a good work out. Cardio on my trigger finger. The look on Telena's face was priceless. She fucked with the wrong bitch. "Drive to 206 Blue Ridge," I demanded Ced.

"You doin' that now too, Sweets?"

"What you think, Ced?"

No more words needed to be said, he did as I told him. Blue Ridge was two blocks over from Hood.

"Park right in front of the house and cut the lights off."

As he did that, I checked my baby to make sure everything was perfect.

Once the car stopped, I opened the door and got out. We were in front of a blue and white house with a black 745 parked in the driveway. The porch light was on, but I didn't care. I walked the gravel walk way to get to the porch. As I climbed the steps, I said a short prayer.

"God, protect me." I hadn't even done a background check on the nigga. Too late now. It was happening.

I breathed in and out slowly before I lifted my hand to bang on the door.

Bam. Bam. Bam.

I had my baby tucked in the back of my pants, under my shirt.

There was no answer, so I banged again, harder that time.

Bam. Bam. Bam.

I glanced at the street to see Ced looking at me. As I turned to walk away, the door flew open.

The word handsome didn't even do the man in front of me any justice. He was drop-dead gorgeous. I was stuck.

"How may I help you?" he asked me as I stood there.

His voice broke the spell I seemed to be under and my wits came rushing back to me.

"My man says *fuck you.*"

He looked at me like I had two heads, but I knew Quick wouldn't be quick enough to duck these bullets. I pulled my baby from the back of my waistband and smoked his ass.

That nigga back there disrespected my man and by doing that he had to pay with his life, beautiful or not.

Jamaica

Chapter 27
Wednesday

"I heard what you told that nigga before you sent his ass to meet his maker." Ced and I were tangled up together as we lay in bed.

I'd heard what he said, but that was the least of my problems. I had to finish my enemies before one of them struck me.

"You hear me, Sweets?"

I looked at him. Yes, I heard him, but I was thinking super hard. I had to find Jay and Dimples, *fast.*

"What did I say?" I finally responded.

"You told him, 'My man says fuck you.'" He must have had the window down.

"What you wanted me to tell him?" I was curious to hear what he had to say.

"Shit, you told him just how I felt."

"Look, I know it's already hard for you not havin' your mother around, so if you don't want me to smoke Steven, now is the time to save him."

A smile was still plastered on his face, and I felt like he may as well be telling me to handle my business.

"It's one thing to be disloyal to me, but to my mom, it's un-live-able."

I knew his heart still hurt for his mother, knowing that she did everything to the best of her ability for his father, and the reward Steven gave her in return was Unforgivable. The pain in Ced's voice was loud and clear to me.

I touched his chest with my left hand and looked up into his eyes.

"With one *disloyal* muthafucka leavin', the world might be a better place."

And just like that, he smiled, and I smiled back. I'd die trying to make that man happy and keep him safe. He knew the love that

I had for him was *real*. He brought my hand to his lips and kissed it before he spoke. "Our love bonds us together forever."

I moved my body in closer to his and lay my head on his chest. I could hear his heart beating slowly. He was so calm when I was around, and I think it was because he knew any problem that he had *would* be taken care of.

I drifted off to sleep in peace with his arms wrapped around me.

***

"Baby, wake up." Ced was shaking my shoulder.

"What time is it?" I asked, sitting up in the bed and looking at him.

"3:30pm."

Damn. I'd been asleep all fucking day. "What's wrong?"

"Bella has been callin' you for thirty minutes straight." As soon as the words left his mouth, I was out of bed. All kind of thoughts were running through my fucking head as I got dressed.

My phone rang again and I answered on the first ring.

"Hello?"

"Ma, what you doin'?"

Hearing Beauty's voice helped me relax. It took a lot of negative possibilities out of the picture.

"I'm just gettin' up. How was school?"

I could hear her breathing hard. She sounded like she'd been running.

"I have a number for you to call."

"Whose number is it, baby?"

"Auntie Dimples." I caught the sarcasm in her voice when she said auntie. "She came to my school today to see me."

By then I was completely dressed and I had my best friend in one hand. Ced was looking me up and down, clearly trying to figure out what the hell was going on.

"What did she say to you?" I kept my voice calm and even, but I was so fucking mad. I swear steam must've been coming off my forehead.

"She said to tell you to make sure you call her ASAP."

"Did she touch you or anything?"

"Naw ma, I'm straight .I just wish I'd had my best friend with me."

Angry or not, that made me smile because I knew she would've used it too.

"What's the number?"

I heard paper crumpling and then she read the number off to me. "336-731… and grandma wants to talk to you, too?"

"A'ite, I love you and be good. Put grandma on the phone."

"I love you, too."

What the fuck? I know Dimples' heart ain't grown that big overnight for her to get that close to my child. She knows I don't fucking play when it comes to Beauty. Is this bitch testing me?

Bella came to the phone and we talked for ten minutes about the whole situation. I told her to keep Beauty home from school the next day, and she agreed that was for the best.

As I replayed the conversation to Ced, his face drew up into a scowl, showing nothing but anger. I was mad at myself for letting that bitch live so damn long.

"Fuck," I said out loud as I dialed the number Beauty had given me.

The call was answered on the first ring.

"Hello?" The sound of her voice made me sick.

"So you brave enough to go to my child's school to give her your number?"

"Well, hello to you too, Sweets," she laughed into my ear.

My breath came fast and I could feel my blood pressure going up.

"Bitch, don't act like we cool," I reminded her ass.

"Bitch, we used to be," she screamed back at me.

"Meet me Thursday at midnight by your fuckin' self on Park Lane, and I mean by your fuckin' self." She ended the call after giving me her orders.

"She'll *never* win, 'cause she has nothing in life to gain, so you can add her to my list," I said over my back as I headed to the kitchen, leaving Ced in the bedroom. I hadn't talked to Traymon in a couple of days, so I figured I'd hit him up as I made us something to eat.

"Baby daddy, what's good with you, nigga?"

I had him on speaker phone since I was cooking and both of my hands were full. Ced was leaning on the wall watching me.

"Baby Ma, I'm chillin'. How our daughter doin'?"

"She's good, probably missin' you. You should call Bella's phone and talk to her."

"I'mma do that, how you doin' though?" He was always gonna be concerned when it came to me. Ced's face was unreadable.

"I'm good, just chillin', you know."

"That's what's up." He took a deep breath before he spoke again.

"I just want to tell you thank you for everything."

Ced was smiling and I wondered what for.

"Don't even mention it."

"I just want you to know that. I'm not gonna hold you any longer, so holla at me when you can, Sweets."

I could tell that he didn't want to get off the phone.

"A'ite." I ended the call before Traymon said something crazy.

"What are you smilin' at?" I cocked my head to the side looking at Ced.

"I'm smilin' 'cause you belong to me *forever*!"

I reminded him of his own words, "One nigga's mistake 'caused you to have my heart."

He didn't reply. He just walked away laughing at me.

***

"I'ma handle this one by myself, and please don't worry, I'm comin' back home to you." I pulled my Timbs on one foot at a time.

Black dickies had become my favorite outfit after all. I felt *untouchable* when I was in all black.

"Don't make me come look for you either," he said before he left me to my business.

My black G-Shock said it was time to roll. It was 12:45 in the morning, and I was ready to bounce. I checked my P89 one more time to make sure one was already in the head of the chamber. I tucked it in the waistband of my pants, behind my back, and I let my shirt fall over it.

As I closed the door behind me and glanced around to see if I saw anything suspicious.

Everything was calm, quiet, and normal.

I was so glad that Ced had that spot over there, and he'd even gotten his father an apartment close to him, so there was no need for a car. I'd just use my feet on this journey.

As I walked over to the other apartment complex, I enjoyed the silence, along with the nice breeze. It was April, so the weather wasn't too hot or cold. It was just right. I reached my target in less than five minutes.

Steven lived on the ground floor in 906, so I didn't need to climb the stairs.

I knocked on the door with my black leather gloves on. There was no answer, so I put my ear to the door to see if I could hear any movement inside. I didn't hear anything. I knocked again, and the door opened before I had to knock a third time.

Suddenly, he was standing in the doorway in a robe, looking at me up and down.

"May I come in?"

He looked at me like I was drunk, crazy, or both.

"Yes, you can." He moved out the way to let me in.

I remembered his place so *well*. It was where I almost died, and thinking about it made me sick. He closed the door and walked in front of me, leading me to the living room.

The apartment smelled clean. Pictures of Ced and Jay were hanging on the walls, along with a few of Ced's mother.

"What brings you here this time of night?" he asked me as he took a seat on the all-white sofa.

I looked around, and things still looked exactly the same as they did the last time I was there. My eyes locked on Jay's picture and my heart beat fast.

"I don't condone the fuckery, foolery, disloyalty, and non-sense that's goin' on today. I'm clearly in a class that no longer exists, and I'm good with that."

I took my eyes off the picture and leveled them on Steven, his facial expression said that he was at a loss as to what I was talking about.

I kept going, hoping that he'd pick up. I would have hated for him to die confused.

"Morals, values, integrity, and honor have become foreign words to most people, but not all. I live by mine all the way. Correct me if I'm wrong, but back in the day your wife held you down. She was a gangsta to the fullest."

He nodded his head up and down, knowing that everything I was saying was one hundred percent fact, but I didn't give him any time to comment. "I salute nothin' but *realness*. I live, breathe, and stand by the ones that I love. I'll even *die* for them."

He opened his mouth to speak, but I lifted my left hand up, telling him to hold on.

"I'm not here to judge you." I put my right hand behind my back and pull the P89. His eyes were big. He'd never expected this. As my baby was pointed at him, I continued speaking my mind. "But I'm here to destroy you." I said, letting three shots off into his body.

Pow! Pow! Pow!

One to the head, one in the chest, and one in that dick of his since he wanted to sling it everywhere. Little pieces of flesh and bone littered the room and the coppery smell of blood filled the air.

As I left, I took one good look at Jay's picture. At one point, I was in love with him, but now he's my most wanted enemy. I closed the door and enjoyed the fresh air that hit my face.

Ced was up playing the X-Box 360, with his .45 on his lap. He smiled when he saw my face, and I winked back, leaving him to finish his game as I headed to the shower.

I knew I had to get the fuck out of Lynchburg when all this shit was over and done with. I might just move back to New York and start all over. I could take trips back and forth so Beauty could see her daddy's side of the family.

It was a thought.

Jamaica

Chapter 28
Thursday

I'd spoken to Beauty earlier. She'd said she'd talked to her father and she couldn't wait until tomorrow for me to pick her up so she could see Ced and the kids. She missed us and we missed her too, but I was still tying up loose ends.

There I was at 10pm, parked on Park Lane Street, waiting on Dimples to show up. So what if I was two hours early? I had to get the drop on this treacherous bitch, and I meant to. Ced, Clap, and Trigger were out there too, all in different vehicles. Ced was parked at the very beginning of the street, Clap was at the end of the block, and Trigger was on Park Avenue, the main street that she had to turn off of to get on Park Lane. I'd know when she turned onto the street. I was parked dead in the middle of the block in an all-white crown Vick with the engine idling, listening to Young Jeezy's *Bury Me A G* track. The street probably had a good ten houses on the block. The street lights were out, but some houses had porch lights on.

My body was in need of some good rest. I adjusted my seat and laid back. I knew if something happened, those niggas would have my back.

My eyes were closed.   I had a feeling that someone besides Ced and Clap was watching me, but my eyes were so heavy I couldn't open them up.

"Sweets, you've turned into a *cold hearted monster*."

"This is what happened 'cause you told me to turn my *heart cold* to protect my life. You programmed this into my brain, King."

"I never knew you would actually turn out this bad."

My brother looked the same, his hair was long, even though it was braided straight back. He was in all white from head to toe.

"Ain't no time to half step the game then, so you better make all your enemies suffer," he told me as he disappeared.

I jumped up. Damn, that was a crazy dream, full of nothing but news that I needed to complete. Kill all my *enemies*. New Mission.

My phone rang. It was Trigger, and that meant Dimples was turning onto the street. I glanced at the numbers glowing on the dashboard. 12:01. The bitch was late.

"Yo."

"Get ready."

I ended the call and checked my baby again. Loaded.

My phone rang again immediately. It was Ced.

"Be on point."

"You know I'm already ready."

I could see the light coming from a vehicle ahead of me. I could tell that there was only one person in the car. As it got closer, I kept my eyes glued to it. My phone rang and I answered it without even looking to see who was calling.

"Hello?"

"Where are you?" Dimples asked.

"I'm where you told me to meet you at."

"Well, I'm here."

She didn't even see me, and I bet she didn't see Ced or Clap either. She was a dumb bitch for real. I watched her park the car five cars behind me on the left hand side.

"I see you," I told her.

"Well, are you gonna come talk to me?"

I was a woman, and a bad one at that, so if it was my time to go, I was going out with a bang. But her voice didn't sound like she'd come to fight. She sounded like she wanted peace.

"Yea." I ended the call and checked my baby one more time. I tucked my baby in my lower back. I left the engine running, and as I stepped out of the car, I wondered again why I didn't just kill that bitch to begin with.

I walked like a Boss because I was a fucking Boss. My head was up, and my eyes were locked on Dimples.

As I got closer and closer, I realized how stupid I was for even coming out here to see what she needed when I could have hunted her down my damn self. *Lesson learned.*

I knew she was watching me, and I hoped Ced was too. As I approached the driver side door, I pulled my baby out and aimed it through the window. Her hands were on the steering wheel and it looked like she was in all white.

"No need for that," she said as the window went down.

Who is this bitch? I asked myself.

"I came in peace."

I was not putting my weapon down. I was not stupid.

"Peace, after all the bullshit you've started?" I asked in disbelief.

Her face was straight ahead. "I'm imperfect. Some people's experiences are worse than others. More people than you imagine live pretty painful lives that are punctuated by bright spots of happiness that allow them to get through the dark days."

Mane, here she goes again with this bullshit.

"I just wanted to tell you thank you for showin' me the real meaning of *love.*"

I saw tears running down her cheeks. She removed her right hand from the steering wheel and picked up a silver object.

My baby was still aimed at her head. The silver object in her hand was a gun, a chrome .38. Before I could react, she jammed it in her mouth, cocked it, and pulled the trigger. The sound caused me to jump. I expected a lot of things to happen that night, but not that.

Damn. I ran back to my car. I'd never seen someone take their own life before. I'd always been the one doing the taking.

As I got inside the car, I answered my phone and pulled off. "You good baby?"

"Let's get the fuck out of here," I told Ced and dropped the call.

I put the gas pedal to the floor as I got the hell out of there. I looked back in my rearview mirror and I could see three cars behind me. I was kind of glad Dimples took herself out. She saved me time, effort, and money. On top of that, I didn't have to dispose of what was left of her.

Twenty minutes later, I was parked in Ced's parking lot waiting on him to park beside me. Clap and Trigger had gone their own ways.

When he exited the car, I exited mine also. We walked together to the door.

"You okay?" he asked, and opened the door for me.

"I'll be good when I find Jay." I put my baby on the kitchen table, and grabbed myself a Redbull from the fridge. What a fucking night. All I could do was shake my fucking head.

Chapter 29
Friday

I was so ready to get my daughter. Mane, I was so excited. Steven's body hadn't been discovered yet as far as I knew, but Dimples was found that morning by a stranger. I'd heard it over the news.

"Bella, have Beauty dressed for me. I'll be pullin' up in six minutes."

"Okay."

Ced had to go to his trap house to handle some business for a second, then he'd go and pick his kids up from their mother's house. When we came back from our vacation. I was gonna go hunting for Jay's ass.

Beauty was standing outside as I pulled up. When the car pulled up in front of the house, she took off towards me. Bella was standing in the doorway, smiling. I waved my hand out the window at her and she waved back.

Before she even closed the door, Beauty was all over me, hugging me like she hadn't seen me in years.

"Hey, baby," I said, squeezing her in my arms.

"Ma, I miss you so much."

"I missed you way more." And I meant it. Living a life like mine was amazing. I had people who loved me beyond everything.

After our hugging session, she took a seat and closed her door. I pulled away, heading to the mansion to wait on Ced and the kids.

We talked the entire way home. She was excited about this vacation that we were getting ready to take as a family.

Forty minutes later, we were finally home. I'd really missed that place. The grass needed to be cut, but I figured Ced would do it when we got back.

"Ma, I am gonna go pack my things up," Beauty told me as we entered the house.

"Okay."

She took off running up the stairs to her room.

Lately, I'd been super tired, like my body wasn't getting enough rest. I closed the door, put the keys on the table, and drop face first into the sofa. It felt so good to be home, even though Jay was still on the run.

"So that's how you do, Sweets?"

The voice caused me to jump up, only to be face to face with a .45.

I hadn't seen Jay that close in a very long time, and I must admit that freedom looked good on him. He was in all *black.*

"You never thought I would find you, huh?"

I was speechless, and mad as fuck, because the nigga had caught me slipping for real.

I might be a bitch, but there was *no bitch in my blood.*

"You left me for dead. We made vows to each other under God as one. I bet you haven't even told him that *we* are married?"

As I looked into his eyes, I didn't see what I saw when I married him in jail. All I saw now was hate.

Yea, *we* were married, husband and fucking wife. Four months into our relationship, I took it to another level. I just didn't tell anyone, and I'd die keeping it a secret.

"*No one* knows." Having a gun in my face didn't cause me to crumble.

I'd lived a *real* life, and I'd die *real*.

"Say your prayers."

"Nigga, pull the trigger and get the shit over."

Boom.

Chapter 30
Caught You Slippin'
Beauty

I know this nigga didn't think he was just gonna break into my house and kill my momma. Yea, he really thought that shit, but he forgot about me, and I'm my mother's child.

My mom always had an extra gun in the house. I knew my .22 wasn't going to be enough, so when I got my hands on her .45, I knew I had to bust it right, and that was exactly what I did. I busted Jay's head wide open. The power from the gun caused me to lose my balance so I ended up on my ass, still holding on to that bad boy.

Watching my first body hit the floor made me feel good. I was ready to ride in the streets with Sweets now. I was my mother's keeper.

The look on my mother's face was priceless. I winked at her and spoke my mind, "Like mother, like daughter."

"Beauty…"

I cut her off. "Ma, I think I'm gonna be better, you just witnessed that I *lay it down, too.*

Coming Soon From Lock Down Publications

RESTRAINING ORDER

By **CA$H & Coffee**

NO LOYALTY NO LOVE

By **CA$H & Reds Johnson**

GANGSTA SHYT

By **CATO**

PUSH IT TO THE LIMIT

By **Bre' Hayes**

BLOOD OF A BOSS **IV**

By **Askari**

SHE DON'T DESERVE THE DICK

SILVER PLATTER HOE **III**

By **Reds Johnson**

BROOKLYN ON LOCK **III**

By **Sonovia Alexander**

THE STREETS BLEED MURDER **III**

By **Jerry Jackson**

CONFESSIONS OF A DOPEMAN'S DAUGHTER **III**

By **Rasstrina**

NEVER LOVE AGAIN **II**

WHAT ABOUT US **III**

By **Kim Kaye**

A GANGSTER'S REVENGE **IV**

By **Aryanna**

GIVE ME THE REASON **II**

By **Coco Amoure**

LAY IT DOWN **III**

By **Jamaica**

I LOVE YOU TO DEATH **II**

By Destiny J

Available Now

LOVE KNOWS NO BOUNDARIES **I II & III**

By **Coffee**

SILVER PLATTER HOE **I & II**

HONEY DIPP **I & II**

CLOSED LEGS DON'T GET FED **I & II**

A BITCH NAMED KOCAINE

NEVER TRUST A RATCHET BITCH **I & II**

By **Reds Johnson**

A DANGEROUS LOVE **I, II, III, IV, V, VI, VII**

By **J Peach**

CUM FOR ME

An **LDP Erotica Collaboration**

A GANGSTER'S REVENGE **I II & III**

By **Aryanna**

Jamaica

WHAT ABOUT US **I & II**

NEVER LOVE AGAIN

By **Kim Kaye**

THE KING CARTEL **I, II & III**

By **Frank Gresham**

BLOOD OF A BOSS **I II & III**

By **Askari**

THE DEVIL WEARS TIMBS **I, II & III**

BURY ME A G **I II & III**

By **Tranay Adams**

THESE NIGGAS AIN'T LOYAL **I, II & III**

By **Nikki Tee**

THE STREETS BLEED MURDER **I & II**

By **Jerry Jackson**

THE ULTIMATE BETRAYAL

By **Phoenix**

BROOKLYN ON LOCK **I & II**

By **Sonovia Alexander**

DON'T FU#K WITH MY HEART **I & II**

By **Linnea**

BOSS'N UP **I & II**

By **Royal Nicole**

LOYALTY IS BLIND

By **Kenneth Chisholm**

I LOVE YOU TO DEATH

By Destiny J

<u>BOOKS BY LDP'S CEO, CA$H</u>

TRUST NO MAN

TRUST NO MAN 2

TRUST NO MAN 3

BONDED BY BLOOD

SHORTY GOT A THUG

A DIRTY SOUTH LOVE

THUGS CRY

THUGS CRY 2

TRUST NO BITCH

TRUST NO BITCH 2

TRUST NO BITCH 3

TIL MY CASKET DROPS

Coming Soon

TRUST NO BITCH (KIAM EYEZ' STORY)

THUGS CRY 3

BONDED BY BLOOD 2

RESTRANING ORDER

NO LOYALTY NO LOVE